Winner, Text Prize for Young Adult and
Children's Writing, 2009

Notable Book, CBCA Young Adult Fiction, 2011

Shortlisted, WA Premier's Book Awards
for Young Adults, 2011

Shortlisted, Gold Inky Award, 2011

PRAISE FOR LEANNE HALL
AND *THIS IS SHYNESS*

'Refreshingly original, Hall's debut novel has a
genuine edge. It's *Bladerunner* meets *Peter Pan*
with a bit of sweetness, sadness and tension.'
Sunday Age

'I loved *This Is Shyness*. It's a world-tilting romance
full of comic-strip cool.' Simmone Howell

'Hall's vision, channelled through her characters
Wolfboy and Wildgirl…is sophisticated, funny and
dead on. Their nocturnal meanderings, bizarre
encounters and burgeoning romance are handled
with unusual skill. *This Is Shyness* is not so much a
work of fantasy as a novel that works by fine-tuning
the ordinary to illuminate its oddness…Hall [is a]
writer with incredible talents.' *West Australian*

Queen of the Night

QUEEN
OF THE
NIGHT

LEANNE HALL

TEXT PUBLISHING MELBOURNE AUSTRALIA

The paper used in this book is manufactured only from wood grown in sustainable regrowth forests.

textpublishing.com.au

The Text Publishing Company
Swann House
22 William Street
Melbourne Victoria 3000
Australia

First published in 2012 by The Text Publishing Company

Cover design by W.H. Chong
Text design by Susan Miller
Typeset by J&M Typesetting
Printed and bound by Griffin Press

National Library of Australia Cataloguing-in-Publication entry

Hall, Leanne Michelle, 1977-
Queen of the night / Leanne Hall.
1st ed.
ISBN: 9781921758645 (pbk.)
For young adults.
A823.4

This project has been assisted by the Australian Government through the Australia Council for the Arts, its arts funding and advisory body.

This book is printed on paper certified against the Forest Stewardship Council® Standards. Griffin Press holds FSC chain-of-custody certification SGS-COC-005088. FSC promotes environmentally responsible, socially beneficial and economically viable management of the world's forests.

For Mum and Dad

one

There's no point fighting.
The hands clamped over my eyes close out the sunlight,
reducing the world to a distant place that glows as if it's
on fire. Without sight, everything else becomes clearer: the
wispy breeze and the crushed grass and the car pulling out
of a driveway, far in the distance. My captor's hot breath
hits me in the face. Strawberry yoghurt and apples.

'No peeking, Jet-ro!'

Diana presses harder, until light flashes behind my
eyelids. Just how vice-like can a five-year-old's grip be?

'Enough!' I shake my head until her fingers loosen.
'I already promised I wouldn't look.'

'You have to count now.' Diana's voice fades as she

moves away. I keep my eyes closed but I know she's creeping backwards with her finger shushing herself, like a pantomime actor.

'This is the last time—' I fit in, before she's away. Her feet pad across the tanbark, her excited breath matching her excited footsteps, right to the edge of the playground. And then she's gone, too far away for me to hear.

I don't count to a hundred. I used to. Now I wait a few minutes, sitting on the warm metal roundabout. Even though it's late in the afternoon the sun still bites. I bet I'm burnt again. Too much of this and I'll start to look like I'm from the City. In Shyness, you can tell a Local by the paleness of their skin.

When I think it's been long enough I yell, 'Ninety-seven, ninety-eight, ninety-nine, A HUNDRED.'

I open my eyes. The scuffed bark around the jungle gym shows a clear path towards the Shyness side of the park. She always drifts in that direction, no matter which game we're playing. I begin to stroll, whistling loudly so she knows where I am.

'Am I warm?' I call out.

Silence. Beyond the playground is a vast expanse of green. There's an oak tree in the far corner that's wide enough to stand behind. Or maybe the player's shelter on the edge of the football field. It looks empty from here, but if she was smart—and she is—she could curl up on the bench and I wouldn't be able to see her feet.

'I'm coming to get you!'

I hear a faint laugh from the direction of the oak. I reach the grass and start to roar in what I think is an ogre-like way. Diana likes it when I howl, but that can't happen in the blistering sunshine. I don't howl as much as I used to.

A pink and red blur darts out from behind the tree and heads for the road.

Crap. No matter how many times I tell her to stay on this side, Diana always gets drawn towards Shyness. I begin to run. There's no point yelling out. She's not supposed to cross that road alone, and she knows I'm going to chase her.

I hurdle a park bench and capture ground quickly, but Diana is already at the edge of the road, looking back to see me coming. She squeals in that way she does when she can't tell if it's still a game. I'm close enough to see the rainbows on her gumboots when the shadows midway across the road wrap themselves around her, swallowing her whole. The squealing stops. I slow as I reach the road.

'Diana, I'm going to tickle you to death when I get hold of you!' I don't sound nearly as fierce as I should and I don't threaten to tell her mum. She may only be five, but Diana recognises an empty threat. Ortolan insists that we play only in Panwood, so that Diana gets as much light as possible, but always, always, she tries to cross into the dark, into Shyness, a suburb where the sun hasn't risen

3

for over three years. A suburb most normal people would like to forget. The twenty-four-hour dark hides a motley population: Dreamers, dropouts, orphaned Kidds, me. I've lived there all my life, and I can't ever imagine leaving.

I feel the Darkness sizzle on my bare arms. The night folds over me, cool and dim, and I can instantly breathe easier. Back again. I pause at the edge of the forest, lifting my head to listen and sniff. Nothing. Dirt and chipboard and paint but no Diana. Someone nearby is cooking sausages. I walk further in, cutting a diagonal path through the trees until the road is no longer visible.

The forest sprang up only a few months ago, the work of an anonymous group of people rather than nature. Overnight, hundreds of fake, two-dimensional wooden trees in varying shapes and sizes, some plain pine and others painted black, appeared in a vacant lot, hammered into the ground. They even scattered shredded wood over the ground to make a floor that's like soft pine needles underfoot.

No one could figure out how they managed to set it up so quickly. It's not up there with the pyramids or Stonehenge, but it was still an impressive feat. I abandon my straight line, and start walking faster, making bigger and bigger circles. The forest isn't huge; I should come across her soon.

'Diana…how 'bout a cheesy roll on the way home?'

No reply.

There's a scuffle behind me. I spin around, examining the forest. The plain pine cutouts stand forward, pale in the night, and the darker trees recede into shadow. I blink. My sense of perspective is thrown right out. I pass a tree with a resident cardboard owl that has foil pie tins for eyes. The forest is unsettling. I could almost swear I smell pine needles.

Just when I am about to yell again there's a familiar giggle to my right. About time.

'Give me a clue,' I say to the trees.

'Wooo-ooooh...Wolfboy, Wolfboy,' Diana hoots from close by. The sound comes from up high, as if she's climbed one of the trees. Some of them have cutout footholds and rungs to encourage people. If she falls and hurts herself I'll be off babysitting duty for good.

'Game's over, Diana!' I use the bad uncle voice. 'Get your bum out here NOW!'

I take another few steps and there she is, leaning against a tree with her arms crossed. I'm about to give her a dressing down when I see that she looks scared.

'Who's afraid of the big bad wolf?' Diana sings in a wobbly voice. Her red sun-visor has slipped down to her neck, and there's mud on her knees. My bad-uncle act was too convincing. I smile at her to show I'm not really mad.

'Why have you always got to run off, Flopsy?'

'I like it here.'

5

I take her grubby hand and walk her towards the road, and back to Panwood. She doesn't resist. She must be hungry after all. The sun dawns over us again as I tell her off. 'You know the rules.'

'You like it there too. You're a *creature of the dark*.'

I snort. Her hand squirms in mine.

'But you're getting lighter, aren't you? You were hairy-scary when I first met you, but now you're not.'

I baulk at this, even though she's right. I don't feel as hairy-scary anymore. Or, at the very least, whatever was happening to me has slowed down.

'Diana, I have to obey your mum's rules. If she says to stay on the other side of the road, then that's what we do, okay? And I don't like that forest anyway.'

'It's bigger on the inside than it is on the outside.'

'Hang on.' I stop and fix Diana's visor so it shields her face. I use the hem of my t-shirt to wipe her knees clean.

'The bird told me a secret,' says Diana, her hands on my shoulders for balance. 'It sang it right in my ear.'

'Make sure you don't tell anyone,' I reply. 'Secrets are for keeping. Come on.' I let Diana crawl onto my back.

The sun is finally dropping below the treeline and losing its daytime heat. I gallop past the bakery before Diana can call me on the cheesy roll, and turn into their street. She reaches to rub her hands over my stubble, a favourite pastime.

'Hey! Don't wipe your nose on me! I felt that!'

'Did not, Jet-ro.'

As we draw closer to the shop I see someone standing on the opposite footpath, looking at it. An older guy who's grey all over: hair, suit, skin. Not Ortie's usual customer. I walk straight up to him to let him know he's been seen.

'It's by appointment only. The number's on the window.'

The man turns to me slowly, as if I've broken a deep concentration. He has a port wine stain filling one eye socket. His suit looks expensive. Diana slips off my back and hides behind my legs. Her visor jabs into my thighs.

'I was struck by the building actually. It's a fine example of the late Victorian style. Beautiful lacework.'

I look sharply at him and then at Birds In Winter, which is a fairly ordinary Panwood terrace, and not in great repair either. I suppose he could be an architect. He's wearing a skivvy under his suit jacket for one. I shouldn't be surprised that property people are still chasing pieces of Panwood. Within a year of the Darkness descending on Shyness, young professionals started to move into the neighbouring suburbs. Close enough for them to maintain the illusion of grungy youth, but not too close to real danger.

Not Ortolan though. She grew up in Shyness, streets from where we lived. She and my brother, Gram, were high-school sweethearts and Diana was the result. She moved back here to bring up Diana close to Gram's memory.

7

'Do you live up there?' he gestures to the first floor. His irises are pure black. Darkitect, I think to myself. I almost answer him, but then I catch myself. He asked so smoothly I almost forgot that I don't owe him anything. Authority clings to him. He reminds me of my dad. He turns a crisp white envelope over in his hands.

'We've got to go.' I pick up Diana, who has gone still and quiet, and march her to the front door.

While I've never seen Ortolan looking less than perfect outside the house, in her studio is another matter. Today she has a pencil stuck behind each ear, and wears a pyjama top over long johns with holes in the knees. 'Is that four hours already?'

Diana flies from my grasp and hurls herself at Ortie, instantly revived. 'I was naughty!'

'Were you just? Why am I not surprised? You look exhausted, Jethroh.'

'She ran me into the ground. I don't know how you do it on your own.' Give me a couple of hours with Diana, and I feel as wrecked as if I've been on a three-day bender.

'But I don't do it on my own. I've got you now.' She sets Diana down on the ground and straightens her dress out.

I grab an apple from the bowl on the workbench and bite into it to hide how pleased I am. It's not just me who thinks I'm part of the family.

'I was drawing those!'

'You're making clothes that look like apples?'

'I want to be an apple,' says Diana. 'I could have a leaf for a hat.'

Ortolan kisses her forehead. 'Are you staying for dinner, Jethro?'

'Nah, I've got rehearsal.'

'Grab some carrot cake. You don't have any food at home, do you?'

'Why would I have food when I can come over here?'

I cut myself a chunk of cake and alternate bites of apple and cake. Tastes pretty damn good.

'Not bad,' I say through my mouthful. 'Am I mistaken or is there sugar in this? Where from?'

Sugar has been scarce for years in Shyness. Even in the adjoining suburbs people are reluctant to sell it, on account of the way it attracts Kidds. The Kidds live on their own in Orphanville—an old housing estate down by the river. Most of the trouble in Shyness is made by the Kidds, not least because they're half-nuts on sugar.

'If I told you that then I'd have to kill you.' Ortie rolls up her papers and ties them with a piece of string. 'Not really. It's back on the shelves, that's all. Did you remember I have that dinner thing tomorrow?'

I do remember. I don't have many things to remember, and babysitting Diana is definitely the most important event in my schedule. 'Six-thirty,' I say.

'That's right. And I don't mean six-thirty Shyness time. And then I definitely owe you a meal. What are you doing the night after?'

'Saturday? Coming over here, I guess.'

Diana reaches up as I squat down, and I receive a sloppy kiss on my cheek. 'Bye, Flopsy.'

The sky is streaky when I let myself out into the street, and the architect is nowhere to be seen. I walk quickly towards the night.

The Shyness side of Grey Street is as derelict as ever, a mouthful of rotting teeth. Most of the buildings here would be condemned if we had a local council to bother.

I stop at the side of the old milk bar. A new billboard dominates the top half of the brick wall. Doctor Gregory looks soulfully into the distance. Fluffy clouds float around his head. 'Dream a little dream...' is printed in large type, along his line of vision. The new poster must only be days old because the Kidds haven't been along to paint KIDDS RUSH IN across it. Though the Kidds have gone quiet recently.

I scowl at Doctor Gregory's orange tan, pomaded hair and sultana eyes, as irritated as if he was standing right before me. He's the worst Shyness has to offer. I have to remind myself that even though his face is plastered all over he can't get to me unless I let him.

I flip him the finger and walk away.

2

I can tell straightaway I'm dealing with a high-maintenance customer. Strolling the aisles in click-clack heels, picking at the clothes with a look on her face that says none of it's good enough for her. I busy myself with Dulcie the mannequin, struggling to pull a ski suit off her armless body.

There's a delicate cough behind me. I ignore it, and concentrate on pulling a blouse over Dulcie without snagging any sequins. Coughing in my ear doesn't exactly equal asking for help. It's amazing how many people don't realise that.

'I'm going to leave my bags here, okay?' the girl says belatedly, after she has already dumped her twenty billion shopping bags on an armchair.

I nod. She's obviously been on an all-day shopping frenzy. She's around my age, so god knows how she can afford all that stuff.

'Have you got anything in smaller sizes?'

I sigh and abandon Dulcie, who looks pissed off that I've left her with one plastic boob out and no arms. 'That whole rack at the end is Japanese vintage. You'll find most of it is pretty small.'

I leave her to browse and peer over the edge of the balcony. Ruth is dusting the record shelves downstairs. It must be nearly closing time. She's dressed head to toe in autumn colours to match her red hair. She sees me and waves me down with a Chux. I try to mime to her that I have a customer upstairs.

'What?' she yells. 'You have a pet moose?'

I make a pair of antlers out of my fists and position them on either side of my head. Then I grab Dulcie's loose arms and slap them together in front of my body, making my best walrus sounds.

'Where's your change room?' asks Miss High Maintenance behind me.

I point to the far corner of the mezzanine with a plastic arm, refusing to lose my dignity. The girl hauls an armful of clothes into the cubicle. 'Can you watch my bags?'

As if I don't have anything better to do. I decide to leave Dulcie au naturel overnight, and instead straighten the racks near the change room. I'm just wondering if I can peek inside Miss High Maintenance's designer bags, when she struggles from behind the curtain. I have to swallow a gasp.

She's wearing the Japanese Princess Dress.

The JPD has hung, unwanted, on the racks for the entire time I've worked here, which must be four months now. No one has ever looked at it, except to laugh at how OTT it is. It's a riot of salmon taffeta, with a high neck, puffy sleeves and a waist that makes a deep V. There are ruffles on the skirt hem, lace windows at the collarbone, and the whole thing is scattered with seed pearls and crystals.

'You don't have a mirror?'

I drag the standing mirror out into the open. I'm enjoying the sight too much to take offence at her demanding tone. To my surprise she swivels in front of the mirror, gazing at her reflection approvingly. I bite my lip to keep from smiling. The colour is terrible on her. She could have been dead for ten days. In the water.

'I don't know...' she says. 'I love it, but I don't normally wear skirts this full.'

'It's all in the accessorising,' I tell her, snatching up a nearby belt and looping it around her. 'You have a tiny waist so you should pull it in tight, like this. You look great. Not many people can pull off this look.'

The girl nods. I should change my job title to Retail

Psychologist and get some impressive letters after my name. And a pay-rise. The not-many-people-can-work-this-look thing gets them every single time, not to mention the word 'tiny' in relation to any body part except boobs. The girl tears herself away from her reflection, her mind made up.

'I'll take it.'

'Excellent choice.'

I carry her bags down the stairs. On the ground floor Helen struggles with a late delivery, signing the invoice, counting the boxes and trying to get the storeroom door open all at the same time.

I ring up the dress. 'Seventy dollars.' I subdue the JPD enough to fit it into a carry bag. Ruth slides behind me and puts the duster back underneath the counter.

The girl hands me a gold credit card. Out of a lingering habit I'm trying really, really hard to break, I check the bank name on the front of the card, even though I haven't seen another FutureBank card since that night in Shyness. But it's just a regular old credit card for a run-of-the-mill rich girl.

I staple the receipts together and drop them in with the dress. 'Enjoy.'

'Thanks,' the girl says, finally, and smiles, happy with her purchase. She looks almost sweet.

Ruth leans on the counter next to me, and we watch the girl struggle out of the shop with her billion-and-one bags.

'Turn that sign over!' Helen calls from the depths of the storeroom. 'I want to get out of here on time. I haven't even cashed up yet.'

'She bought the Princess Dress.' Ruth sounds like she's seen Jesus burnt into a piece of toast.

'Uh-huh.' I try not to sound smug. I sound extremely smug.

'That's exactly why I hired this girl.' Helen backs out of the storeroom and squeezes my shoulder. 'No retail experience, but I could tell straightaway she's got the Midas touch. You two take off now. I'm nearly done here.'

Ruth leaves to meet her boyfriend Duncan while I switch off the lights.

'Oh, Nia, before you go.' Helen is out of breath from moving the heavy boxes, her long dark hair mussed. 'There's a special customer coming in tomorrow, but I'm not sure what time. I've kept aside some things for her in this tub, okay?'

'What does she specialise in?'

'Anything black and funereal. She drops in every few months. Nice woman.'

'Gotcha,' I say.

The sun is sinking by the time I walk down Mayfield Street. It's the nicest part of the day when I finish, when the light is turning golden and soft, and the temperature has dropped enough to walk without sweating up a storm.

I put my headphones in as I reach the station, relying on my music to keep the world at bay.

The train rattles through the tunnel under the river and then shoots through the industrial zone towards Plexus. The Emporium is miles from my house. All up, it takes me about forty-five minutes one-way. Everyone in the carriage looks crumpled and tired and sweaty. A little kid starts to whine. I turn the volume higher, until guitars and synths fill my ears.

I first heard Dreamer rock in this crazy underground club in Shyness, on the night I met Wolfboy. I still can't think of him as Jethro. A couple of months ago curiosity got the better of me, and I hunted for some Dreamer rock, not even sure if it existed outside Shyness. Turns out there's a whole world of it out there, online. Turns out I actually don't mind the stuff. I downloaded the perfect soundtrack for the long commute. One good thing to come out of that night.

I thought there would be more. I wouldn't have said that about an ordinary one-night hook-up, but nothing about that night was ordinary. Not meeting Wolfboy, not getting mugged by the Kidds, not breaking into Orphanville to get his brother's lighter back, not the rooftop showdown with the creepy Doctor Gregory. Not the feeling that we were just two stars in the endless night sky, as dazzling and dwarfed and stupendous and insignificant as that made us. I let my guard down with Wolfboy, and I think he did the same with me. I like to think that I'm a good judge of people, but I guess I'm not.

At first Dreamer rock reminded me too much of Shyness, but I'm over that now. Now the music is only a tool to take me someplace else. I've trained my brain not to think about things that are not worth thinking about.

We express through Southside Station and, as always, I hold my breath as we pass my old school and look the other way, out over terracotta roof tiles and other people's backyards. That school and those mean girls are in the past, along with so many other things from that time. I thought I'd have to wait until I finished school and moved out to change my life, but then I decided to start changing it immediately.

My job at the Emporium has been one of the best things to ever happen to me. A far cry from the days of slimy Neil and the call centre. But my final year of school starts next week and Mum has ordered me to cut down on my shifts, even though I know she's grateful for the extra money I bring in. I haven't spoken to Helen about it yet. I'm scared she'll tell me she can't fit me on the roster at all if I can't do weekdays.

The train has emptied by the time we reach Plexus. The ugly towers of the Commons stick up above the skyline. Lights are beginning to ping on through the grounds.

I pull my earbuds out when I go through the gate and skirt the crowded basketball court.

'Baby!' yells someone from the knot of players, provoking a wave of shouted suggestions, some coming from kids too young to even know what they're suggesting. I flip them the finger and watch them turn.

'Bitch!' screeches a boy, clinging to the wire fence.

I move to the fence so he can see I'm not scared. 'Make up your mind,' I say through the wire. 'Am I your bitch or your baby?' I throw an imaginary ball at his face, and laugh when he drops backwards off the fence. I walk fast, not too fast, to my building.

Mum is in the kitchen gathering together her handbag, her textbooks, and trying to tie her hair back.

'Shouldn't you have left already?'

'I know, I know. I got held up making soup for you.'

'I told you, I can feed myself.'

Mum kisses me on the cheek. She smells of this disgusting peach perfume I've been trying to wean her off for years. 'I just want to do things properly, darling. Message me before you go to bed.'

Sometimes I don't recognise this new mum, who cooks dinner and goes to night classes at TAFE and checks up on me constantly. She even looks like a student in the new jeans I helped her pick out. 'Don't worry. I'll be on the couch all night with my Lit reading.'

'Good. Don't stay up too late.'

I hand her a mandarin from the fruit bowl. She stops at the front door. 'Oh, I checked the train times today. You'll have to meet me at Central Station straight after school on Wednesday.'

'Ma, I wasn't joking when I said I'm not going to skip school in the first week. Go on your own to Fish Creek.'

'But you never see your aunt. And what about your cousins?'

I feel like banging my head against the wall. She always springs this stuff on me just as she's leaving the house. 'First you carry on about marks and homework and university, then you try to pull me out of school for two days. The only reason you want me to come is because you're scared you and Aunt Shell will wind up throttling each other as usual.'

'That's not true.'

'It is true.' I push her out the door before she starts going on about the *sacrifices she's made*. 'You're late. Go to class.'

three

I've just hit the steep part of Oleander Crescent when I see the dog under the only working street light. Its back curves in a bony arc as it fusses over something on the ground.

It turns to me with silvery eyes and flattened ears, before taking the thing in its mouth.

'What have you got there, boy?'

The dog shakes its head so fast I can't see what's clamped between its teeth.

I creep closer. 'Drop it.'

The dog turns its back to me and steps out of the light. I try another tack.

'Fetch!' I throw my apple core past the streetlight, onto

the verge. The dog thinks for a few seconds. Eventually he leaves his prize and walks over to sniff the apple core.

I swoop in.

It's a dead tarsier, curled up on the ground, hind legs sticking out at an unnatural angle. I prod it with my foot. The dog must have chanced upon it, because it looks intact. No blood or innards in sight. What could have killed it?

There's a lawnmower rumble to my right, a long gravelly warning. The dog stalks towards me, eyes flashing, hackles raised. I bare my teeth and let loose my own growl. To my surprise I have no problem coming up with the goods. My rumbling throat feels good. Mine. My dead tarsier.

The dog pauses for an endless moment, while the tension builds. Then it suddenly drops its tail between its legs and whines. I stare it down until it slinks away. When I can no longer see it I turn back to the body.

The fur is surprisingly soft. It looks coarse and wiry, but feels like cotton wool. A mottled mixture of brown and grey. I scoop the animal up, its body still warm.

The house is dark and quiet when I let myself in. Paul isn't in his room, and Thom hasn't arrived. That'd be right. The sun will rise over Shyness before they show up on time for rehearsal. It never used to bother me. But since I've been hanging out with Ortie and Diana I've grown used to being somewhere when I said I would.

Even though there's no sound of amps being dragged over the upstairs floor, the house doesn't have the ringing emptiness it used to.

'Blake!'

'Back here.'

I leave the tarsier on the kitchen bench and poke my head around her door. Blake never closes it. I can't imagine she had much privacy in Orphanville, when she was messed up on sugar and running with the Kidds, and she still doesn't seem to need it. At the same time she rarely ventures upstairs, where my bedroom is. I was worried at first, what it would be like living with a fourteen-year-old girl, but so far it's been no problem at all. Blake is not your typical teenager anyway.

Her room bursts with warm candlelight. The mattress—dragged from Mum and Dad's old room—takes up at least two-thirds of the floor space. Down the spare wall are bookshelves we made out of planks of wood and bricks. Blake sits on her bed, surrounded by books and notebooks and pillows.

'Power off again?' The house is powered from an illegal tap so I don't have to pay bills.

'Patchy,' she says. 'I was getting sick of it going on and off so I decided to stick with candles.'

'What are you working on this week?'

'Fireflies.'

Blake brushes her hair out of her face, and holds up a tatty book. *Nocturnal Insects.* A sketchbook lies open on her bed, filled with drawings of insects. They're pretty good. I keep encouraging Blake to show Ortie her sketches, but she's too shy.

I slide between the bed and the bookshelves, leaning down to scan the hundreds of books.

'Have you got anything about tarsier?'

'Maybe.'

'Tell me again where you got so many books from?' Some of the books look old and valuable. I can't imagine her precious library stored in Orphanville. The Kidds are such pyromaniacs you could never be sure they wouldn't add the books to a bonfire.

Blake doesn't answer. She squints at her shelves. 'I could get you something about them if you're interested.'

'Don't worry too much about it,' I say. 'Come and see this.'

In the kitchen I show her the tarsier. It lies there, still soft, maybe even still slightly warm, looking more asleep than dead, except for its staring eyes. A monkey less than half the size of a possum.

Blake blinks down at it. She pushes her glasses onto the top of her head. 'Oh.' Her breath escapes. 'What happened to it?'

'I don't know. I found it on the street. I can't see

anything wrong with it. I thought you might know.'

Blake gently rolls the tarsier over in her hands. She came in close contact with them all the time when she was with the Kidds. The tarsier are more like colleagues than pets to them. Just as likely as the Kidds to steal, or jump out at you in a dark alley. The perfect nocturnal sidekicks.

Sympathy and scientific interest battle it out on her face. I can see her dissecting the animal with her mind, trying to see what's wrong. If Blake hadn't dropped out of school so young she might have had a chance to study science or zoology at university.

'It looks healthy,' she says.

'Apart from the fact that it's dead.'

'It's underweight. I can feel its ribs.'

'I couldn't think of anyone who could tell us what happened to it.'

There's someone for everything in Shyness. If you want house paint or minigolf or a massage, that's easy. But I can't think of a single doctor or vet, not just here, but even in Panwood. Well, apart from the obvious doctor. And chances are he bought his bogus title on the internet.

'Should we bury it?' Blake asks.

'I suppose. We could find a spot in the backyard.'

'I might pop it in the fridge for a while first. I could take it to my friend and see what she thinks.'

'What friend?'

She shakes her head, then fetches the cling wrap from a drawer and lays a piece out next to the tarsier. I didn't even realise we had cling wrap. It must have been there since Mum bought it. Even now, three years after they left, the ghost of my parents' presence in the house gives me a shiver.

'Why all the secrecy?'

She doesn't answer.

I don't really care. I'm glad Blake has a friend besides me. She should get out more often than she does. I turn away from her wrapping up the corpse. The sight of fur pressed tightly against the clear plastic wrap makes me queasy. I check the fridge. There's not much in there: a bottle of tomato sauce and an onion. I suppose a dead tarsier won't hurt.

'Seen Paul? We're supposed to have rehearsal.'

'Nope.'

I'm not surprised. While Paul has technically been living here since Thom kicked him out of the cottage to make way for his girlfriend, lately it seems as if he's never home. I thought we'd be better friends than ever, living in the same house, but it hasn't turned out that way.

I leave Blake in the kitchen and wander upstairs to call Thom. It sounds as if I woke him up, but Thom always sounds like he just woke up.

''Sup?'

'Rehearsal. It's Thursday night. Rehearsal's what's up.'

'Haven't you spoken to Paul? Rehearsal's off.'

'I haven't seen him for days. Speaking to me isn't high on his agenda. It's nice to know he keeps in touch with you, though.' I push open my bedroom window for air. The band is the only thread keeping us three connected. If we lose that, I don't know what's left.

'Nah, it's not like that. I ran into him on the street, totally random. He said he couldn't make it to rehearsal.'

'Where?'

'Near Umbra. We went to this cool, uh, I guess it was a house party where everyone had to bring something they didn't want anymore, and then you could take home anything you wanted. I got an awesome set of headphones. You should have come.'

Yeah, I might have been up for that if I'd been invited. Before the fact, and not after. I've hung out with Thom and his girlfriend Maggie enough times to know that I'm the appendix of the situation. I look out the window and across darkened rooftops. A long plume of smoke trails from the top of an Orphanville tower. It looks more serious than bonfire smoke. The Darkness is broken along the horizon, a mosaic of black clouds. It's hard to tell if it's light bleed from the city, or the reflection of a larger fire.

I don't like admitting my paranoia to Thom but I have to ask. 'Is he mad at me about something?'

'No, Paul's not mad at you. Why are you asking such dumb-arse questions, Jethro?'

I regret thinking that Thom would be a good person to discuss this with. Maybe I'm paranoid, but it feels as if Paul doesn't look me in the eye anymore on the rare occasions when we do talk.

'Because we've got a show in two days,' I white lie. 'And it'd be nice if we didn't sound like shit for a change.'

'Relax. We don't sound shit.'

'Don't tell me to relax.'

'You never used to care. You'll be awesome. All you've got to do is get your howl on and you sound great.'

'You used to care. Now you just sit on your fat arse with your girlfriend watching DVDs.'

Thom sighs. In the past he would have hung up on me for less than that. 'You need to get some, Jethro.' He sounds sorry for me. 'You should have called that girl.'

My eyes shoot over to Wildgirl's letter blu-tacked to the wall below my favourite Long Blinks poster. Thom doesn't even need to say who he means. How could there be anyone else? I never told Thom and Paul that I did try to call her, the one time.

Thom speaks again. 'I know you've been busy with Ortolan and Diana, but, dude, you're not that busy.'

I hear a muffled voice over the drone of Thom's TV. Someone else offering their unsolicited opinion.

'Is Maggie listening to this?'

'Ah…no.'

I grit my teeth. Thom sighs again. 'Jethro, you sound knackered. Get some sleep and quit worrying about Paul.'

'See you Saturday.' I hang up. My throat itches. Moonbeams want to drag me out the window, but I won't let them. I look more closely at Wildgirl's letter stuck to my bedroom wall. *Nia xx* scrawled at the bottom. Her real name. I know it by heart. I can't call her now. It's been too long.

I pick up my acoustic guitar because that's what I do when there's nothing else to do. I sit on my bed and strum. The chords stream faster as I warm up. I used to call on the Darkness when I played the guitar. But now I close my eyes and the notes are black ribbons spooling from my fingertips, reminding me of Wildgirl's hair.

four

I wake up curled around my guitar like it's a sleeping girl. I push it away from me and sit up, feeling pathetic. If I had any dreams I can't remember them. It's been so long since I've had a proper sleep.

I find my watch next to the bed. It's four, and it must be Friday, but I've got no idea if it's day or night. Regardless, I should leave the house. Nothing good comes of moping around doing nothing.

Blake's bedroom is empty and her bike has gone from the hallway. The insect book is still open on her bed. I rummage through her books, still thinking about the dead tarsier.

There are no Dewey decimal labels on any of the book

spines, so Blake can't have been raiding the abandoned public library. I select a book at random—*Heliographs and Optical Communication*—and look inside. The inside front cover has been stamped with blood-red ink. A curly *W&S*, set inside a rectangle, twined with leaves. An old-fashioned logo, or monogram. I check a few more books— they're all stamped identically—but there's nothing on tarsier.

As I'm piling the books back into the crate, some letters catch my eye. The book is cream-coloured and pamphlet-slim. The title embossed in gold on the plain front cover: *SHYNESS: A young lady's treatise*. By Delilah Gregory. I wonder if she's a relative of the Doctor.

I flick through the book. It's old, and odd, with journal entries and sepia-tinted photographs. Delilah is twenty, but seems much younger. Her journal is as melodramatic as Paul's early poetry. She apparently detested every member of her household, including the housemaid. No one under-stood her. No one cared about what she wanted. I wish Paul was here to see it. Historical artifacts are more his kind of thing.

Paul's bedroom, my parents' old room, is as empty as Blake's, but it has a staler, sourer smell about it, with a thin camping mat and a sleeping bag in the centre of the room. There are still round marks in the carpet where the old bed used to stand. I can't see Paul's satchel anywhere.

I leave the door open to let some air in and head out

into the night. The usual mist hangs near the ground along Oleander Crescent, but when I lift my face I can also smell traces of smoke on the breeze.

It's amazing how the thought of Doctor Gregory can bring on a headache. Even before the night Nia and I came face to face with him in Orphanville, he would harass me with letters about my 'condition'. I had to look up what 'psychosomatic hypertrichosis' meant. Doctor Gregory thinks I'm like this because I'm crazy. The howling, the hair, the appetite, the growth spurt, the muscles—all due to what's going on in my mind.

After that night, after I beat up Doctor Gregory's bodyguards, I expected payback for sure. But so far, nothing.

I take Hobson Street towards Ennio's, the only decent place to get coffee in Shyness. There's a long trickle of people walking in front of me, and, when I turn to check, quite a few behind. Twenty or so people walking in the same direction. Peak hour. This straight stretch of road is lined with two-storey terraces, mostly Dreamer houses. The only reason to be on Hobson is if you live here, or you're going to Ennio's.

I slow my steps, puzzled. Surely not everyone needs a caffeine fix at the same time? The people in front walk metres apart and don't talk to each other, but, despite this, I can't shake the feeling they know each other. They don't look at each other at all, not even with casual curiosity or out of caution. They walk separated by neat regulated distances. A handful are dressed almost identically, in blue cotton pants and shirts.

I turn around, under the guise of checking the rooftops for tarsier, to see that several of the people behind me are also dressed in the blue uniform. I'm caught in a silent street parade. Everyone walks with purpose, eyes straight ahead. Most are youngish, in their mid-twenties, but there is one middle-aged woman among them. They don't seem to notice or care that I'm checking them out. I drop into a crouch, pretending to tie my shoelace. I hope no one realises my boots have zips.

'My boy!' A voice calls out, whispering and urgent. 'Over here!'

Someone stands in the shadowy doorway of the closest house, beckoning furiously.

It's Lupe.

The dark doorway can't hide the unmistakable red puff of hair, or her tropical tent dress. I wait until the last person has passed me, then join her.

'What are you doing here?'

I've never seen her anywhere other than in sight of her van, and here she is on the other side of Shyness, deep in Dreamer territory. She has a thick cardigan over her parrot dress as a concession to the cold, and a battered handbag thrown over her shoulder.

Her dark eyes crinkle. 'I am being the spy.'

'On who?' I ask. 'On me?'

'Always you are thinking you are centre of the universe,' Lupe smiles. 'Not you, my boy—Paul.'

I poke my head out of our doorway to see the tail end of the parade turn the corner.

'I didn't see him.'

'He passed already, before you came. I see him walk with blue people.'

'Let's go then. We can catch up.'

Lupe throws her hands up. 'He has long passed and I'm an old woman. I won't be running all over town.'

'You're not old,' I say, even though she does look shorter and older outside her caravan, without her prize possessions gathered around her. 'What are you doing on Dreamer's Row anyway? How long have you been following him?'

Lupe flaps her hand vaguely. 'I am a few streets away on errand when I see Paul. I think to myself I will talk to him. But then I see the blue people.'

'You mean the way they're dressed?'

While I've never seen people dressed like hospital orderlies before, Locals go through weird phases all the time.

Lupe pats my cheek. 'Not just a pretty face, are you?'

I help her down the stairs. I can see the circle of white on the crown of her head where her hair needs touching up. 'What errands do you have to do?'

'Is all done, my boy.' She pats her bulging handbag.

We start down the street. The middle-aged woman I saw earlier is standing in the yard next door, looking at us. A statue at the fence line. I take Lupe's elbow.

'Evening,' I say, keeping us moving.

The woman comes to life, as if my greeting has activated her. Her face becomes animated and stern. She shakes her finger at us. 'Marcus! How many times have I told you to take off your shoes before you come into the house? Tracking mud everywhere. I just did those floors.'

'Sorry,' I play along. I nudge Lupe. 'I won't do it again.'

'That's right,' says the woman. And then her face changes again. The life ebbs out of it and a confused expression takes over. She looks from me to Lupe.

'You're not him, are you?'

'No, we're not,' says Lupe.

'Slippage,' says the woman. 'It happened again.'

Lupe hesitates, and I make it clear we're leaving. 'Bye now.'

I walk fast towards Grey Street, still with my arm linked through Lupe's. She takes three steps to my one. I catch myself frowning at the ground as I walk. Has Paul really found new friends? Is that why he hardly comes home anymore? I wasn't surprised to be dumped by Thom for Maggie, but I always assumed Paul and I would be tight forever.

34

'Lupe, did you actually see Paul talking to those people?'

Lupe shakes her head. Her face is bright with make-up, her eyes sharp. 'There is no talking but he is one hundred per cent with them.' She grips my arm tightly. 'Our Paul is like lost puppy trying to find family.'

'He's not lost,' I say, trying to sound scornful about the idea, even though I haven't seen him in over a week and if his absences go on much longer he could qualify as lost.

'Jethro, I do not know if your eyes are open but I see Paul and this pretty girl go together for months. And I think to myself, there is youth and there is happiness. But recently I see Paul, and I see no pretty girl.'

I blink. Lupe is in one of her cryptic moods. I know that Paul was seeing this girl a while back, but her name has slipped from my mind. 'I still don't get why you need to spy on him.'

'Because I only see Paul by his self. Not with pretty girl, not with you. Come to see me, on his own. And when I see him, it does not need a doctor to know that he is lost. And now he is with these people and, Jethro, these people are not normal.'

5

On Friday I'm neck-deep in seventies shirts when the door buzzer sounds. I crawl to the edge of the mezzanine and look over, pleased to have an excuse to take in some fresh air. Helen makes sure all our stock is dry-cleaned before it even comes into the store, but there are some things—the chemical reactions that occur when armpits come into contact with polyester, for example—that cannot be erased.

The customer shelters beneath a ruffled black umbrella; the megawatt sun outside is visible even from this position.

'Hey, are you free up there?' Ruth calls out from underneath my feet—she's probably busy with shop regular, Difficult Steve.

I'm about to reply when the words die in my mouth. The customer lowers her brolly, exposing cheeks as pale and perfect as pearls.

I've only met her once but I'd recognise her anywhere. It's Ortolan.

I fall back from the edge of the balcony, suddenly aware of my heart beating in my chest.

I met Ortolan in Shyness, on the night I met Wolfboy. She used to go out with Wolfboy's brother, Gram, and she's pretty much the most stylish, nicest person I've ever met.

'Babe?' Ruth calls out again. 'I need you down here.'

I risk another peek over the edge of the mezzanine. Ortolan is waiting patiently by the counter. Even as I'm panicking, I'm admiring her black outfit, which she no doubt designed and made herself. Her pants taper in sharply at her ankles, and the sun zings off the shiny gold epaulettes on her shoulders.

Ortolan must be the customer that Helen told me about, the woman who likes gothy things. Helen will kill me if I don't take special care of her. And I forgot to tell Ruth about the clothes set aside in the storeroom. When I finally trudge down to the ground level, I have a sheepish look on my face. Ruth is stuck over by the LPs, deep in conversation with Difficult Steve. For the first time ever, I understand the saying 'lamb to the slaughter'. What is she even doing on this side of town?

Ortolan's face brightens when she sees me. 'Wildgirl!'

I wasn't a hundred per cent sure she'd recognise me. We only had a short conversation that night, albeit about the heavy topic of Wolfboy's dead brother.

'I'm Ortolan,' she says, when I don't respond. 'I don't know if you remember—'

'No, of course I do,' I say. 'It's nice to see you again.'

I try to brush down the front of my pants. I've been grubbing around in bags of new stock and I'm covered in dust. Even my face feels coated.

'How long have you worked here? I had no idea. I've been coming to Helen for years.' Ortolan's hair is the same coppery colour but she's had it cut shorter, into a smooth bowl cut.

'Uh, a few months. School holidays.' I come to my senses and move behind the counter. 'Helen left some stock out for you.'

I drag the plastic tub out into the open, bending over awkwardly with my bum in the air. It's hellishly heavy. 'Where do you want to look at this?'

'I don't want to be in your way. How about over by the window?'

There's a long pause when I straighten up. I scramble for something to say while my cheeks flame red. I'd like to run away before Ortolan mentions anything about that night, but I don't want to be rude. Her skin is even more translucent in this light. Faint sea-green veins cross her neck behind her feathered earrings.

'How is Diana?' I ask eventually. I think that was her daughter's name.

Ortolan smiles. 'She's great—a real character. It's frightening how fast she's growing up. You should come over and meet her some…'

Ortolan's voice trails off and she looks at her feet, as flustered as me. She knows, then, that Wolfboy never called me. I wonder how close to Ortolan Wolfboy's become, and what he might have confided in her. For a brief, and stupid, moment I want to ask: How is he? Does he ever mention me? Not ever?

'And business is good?' I say instead; my voice sounds thin. I bend down and flip the lid off the tub.

'It's good. Better than good, actually. I'm so glad you've found a job with Helen, Wildgirl. She really knows her stuff. You'll learn a lot from her.' Ortolan holds a black glomesh top up to the light, appraising it critically.

I choose this moment to back away, while my dignity is still partially intact. 'Let me know if you need anything. I'm just over here.'

I retreat to the front counter, where Ruth joins me.

'Sorry I didn't come downstairs straightaway.' I drag my fingers through a bowl of buttons. I'm already going over things I could have said differently. What if Ortolan reports back to Wolfboy that I'm an awkward freak?

'I would have been fine, but Difficult Steve is in form today.' Ruth is an excellent mimic. 'And was this…uh, Herb Alpert recording…made before or, uh…after he disbanded the Tijuana Brass?'

There's a wracking cough over by the men's shoes. Difficult Steve stands on the other side of the cowboy boots, not ten metres away. His head is barely visible between the shelves, but there's no mistaking that moustache.

'Oh, crap.' Ruth is stricken. 'Oh, I feel awful. Do you think he heard?'

I pat her arm. 'Not unless he has superhuman hearing.'

'I shouldn't make fun of him. He means well.'

'He's got a little crush on you,' I say. 'Duncan had better watch out.'

'Did you hear Helen has talked him into modelling at Shopping Night on Monday night? Duncan that is, not Difficult Steve. You'll be there, won't you?'

'It's my first day back at school but Helen made me promise to come weeks ago.'

Ruth starts unpicking a loose hem. 'You'll love it. All the best customers will be there—no one misses it.'

I look across to where Ortolan is sorting the clothes into two piles. 'So, Ortolan is likely to be there?'

'I'd say so. You don't like her?'

I could lie at this point, but this is Ruth I'm talking

to. Ruth of the homemade cupcakes and the lifts to the train station. Ruth who manages Helen's tizziness and is the mother hen of the Emporium, even though she's only twenty-five, half Helen's age.

'No, she's lovely. But she knows this guy who…someone I used to know.'

Ruth puts down her sewing and fixes me with her clear green gaze. 'This is to do with that howling boy, right?'

I nod, caught out. I'd totally forgotten how chatty I got on my first Friday night drinks with the Emporium crew. Ruth has powers. Together, she and Helen could extract classified information from the toughest spy. Ruth listens with completely genuine interest while Helen asks the cheeky questions. Much more effective than good cop, bad cop. The government really should get in touch with them.

Helen couldn't believe I didn't have a boyfriend, so I told them the bare bones of the story. There's not much to tell, really, especially the ending, which is a real dud. Boy never calls girl. Girl gives up hope.

Now I can't imagine anyone being special enough to get my attention. Helen said it will happen to me again, but I have to be patient. I'm sick of being patient, so here's my new theory: boys can go to hell. I'm going to focus on my schoolwork and get the best grades possible. I don't need anyone or anything to interfere with that.

Ruth is still looking at me, her needle poised in midair.

'But this is your chance to find out why he didn't call you.'

'I can't ask about that!'

In the corner Ortolan gathers together the glomesh top and a few other pieces.

'I couldn't ask that, could I? I'd look like an idiot.'

Ortolan walks towards us.

Ruth backs away. 'I'm thinking there's something I need to check out back…'

'Ruth!' I hiss, and grab her wrist, but she's too fast. The staffroom door bangs behind her. I push aside the buttons, clearing a space on the countertop, and compose myself. Ortolan smiles as she places the clothes in front of me. My face is still on fire.

'A few gems, as usual,' she says.

'Glad to hear it.' I start ringing them up, thankful I've got something to do with my hands.

'Wildgirl, ah…' Ortolan doesn't know where to look, and she's not the only one. 'Ah, I'm not foolish enough to ask Jethro about girl stuff, but—'

'Oh, it's okay,' I jump in. 'You don't need to explain on his behalf. I got the message loud and clear. He wasn't interested. It's okay.'

My feet are telling me to run out the front door and down the street, but I have to stay here and fold clothes. I'm fast becoming a furnace.

'Oh.' Ortolan looks confused. 'I thought…' She stops

42

again. 'I don't mean to pry...I mean, I don't know the details of what happened, other than seeing you two together.' Ortolan blushes, except on her, it just tints her cheeks a delicate pink. 'I'm really messing this up,' she says. 'What I wanted to say was: I'm so glad to see you, and thank you.'

'Thank you?'

'Jethro was different after that night. Whatever you said or did, afterwards he was so much more involved with Diana and me.'

'Oh, I'm sure it's nothing to do with me.'

I did tell him to become better friends with her. Even without knowing everything about the situation, it seemed wrong that Wolfboy wouldn't get to know his niece.

She's finally able to look at me properly. 'Well, I happen to think it has everything to do with you. Whatever happened afterwards. Those two boys, Gram and Jethro ...I don't think talking about feelings was encouraged much in their family.'

'Oh. Right.' It's not the right response, but my head is spinning. Ortolan has brought up a painful topic, something she'd rather not think about, purely to make me feel better.

'You should visit me at my studio, I'd love to see you. Jethro doesn't need to know about it.'

'I'd like that.'

43

Ruth emerges from the staffroom cautiously, just as Ortolan scoops up her bag.

'Thank you, girls,' she says, smiling at me before she leaves.

Something weird happens when I leave work. I go to the station as usual, but when I take the escalators down to the subway platforms I find myself stopping a level early. I'm on a northbound train, in the Friday evening crush, before I'll admit to myself what's going on.

At Panwood I leave the train, swept along in a tide of commuters who soon flow past me and away. After a few minutes of pretending to look at a parched flower clock, I decide that I might as well continue on.

I walk slowly through concrete-bound narrow streets that trap the summer heat. The closer I get, the more the street traffic thins out. Soon I'm walking alone. The turrets of the Diabetic Hotel climb above the buildings and the sight makes me nervous. The Diabetic marks the border, the unofficial gateway to Shyness.

I can still turn back.

This is only the second time I've seen the transition to Darkness during the daytime. The first time I was heading away from the Darkness and Wolfboy, going home after that night. It was early morning and the daylight in Panwood was still dim. Now, though, the summer sun is last-gasp bright at six-thirty, and the difference between Shyness and Panwood is much more obvious.

My heart has risen in my throat and I feel almost dizzy with what I'm doing. What am I doing?

I stand on the light side of Grey Street and look across into the filmy black night that curtains Shyness. Behind me the automatic door of a supermarket opens and closes, disgorging shoppers. I move across Grey Street, each step taking me closer to the night. A strong smell of smoke hangs in the air.

Once I get close, I stop and shut my eyes, breathless with the thought that Wolfboy is on the other side of this boundary. That I'm playing roulette. That he could be walking down the dark side of Grey Street. That he could turn towards the edge of Shyness, and see me.

What are the chances of that happening? Zilch?

I was so sure he was going to call that for the first five days I didn't even worry that he hadn't. Then, after that, every day was torture. I made up excuses for him. Maybe he lost my phone number, maybe Doctor Gregory had kidnapped him, maybe aliens came and took him back to their home planet.

Then, once I'd accepted the awful truth, I pushed him from my mind. I kissed someone else. I concentrated on school. I got over him. And then Ortolan walks into the Emporium, talking about how that night changed him.

I take a deep breath.

A hunched figure shuffles along the footpath on the Shyness side of Grey Street, coalescing out of the gloom. He bends over an overflowing bin, picking through the rubbish. There are no lights on in the shopfronts opposite me. I look up to the telephone lines to see if I can spot any tarsier running overhead, but even they're somewhere else.

The man finds a squashed packet of cigarettes and crows audibly when he finds a lone cigarette left. He shuffles off without looking at me. When I stick my hand into the Darkness it's like easing myself into a cold swimming pool. I take a step forward. The night sucks me across the halfway mark and folds me into its arms. Chills.

I jump back out.

The sun prickles my skin. In the warmth I feel ashamed of my weakness in coming here. I don't care what Ortolan said: Wolfboy has forgotten me. I peel myself away from Shyness, and head towards the things I know.

six

Although Lupe complains, I insist on walking her to her van. Grey Street is as quiet as it ever gets. The trail of blue people has disappeared.

We don't talk much as we walk. Lupe has a calm, pleasant look on her face, as if we're walking through a lovely garden, rather than the decaying street. The supermarket on the Panwood side throws a determined patch of light over the border, but its glow doesn't brighten my mood. I trust Lupe's opinion. If she's this worried about Paul, then I should be too.

Old Jim, one of the Diabetic regulars, shambles past us on Saturnalia Avenue. Jim survived lung cancer five years ago, but I'm not surprised to see him with a cigarette clutched in his clawed hand.

Lupe's van, when it comes into sight, rocks back and forth as if the ground is moving underneath it. But it's not an earthquake causing the commotion.

'Those little shits!' I break into a sprint, leaving Lupe behind. The hazy circle that always envelops her van is gone. She won't be able to see them yet, but there are people-shaped silhouettes standing on the van roof, jumping up and down. Kidds.

Even though I haven't needed to run in months, my legs and arms oblige immediately. My feet whip the ground. As I get closer to the old petrol station where Lupe's van is permanently stationed, I see more Kidds at the base of the van, pushing on the sides. They're trying to topple it off its brick foundations.

I let rip a battle cry that's half-howl, half-swear word. A Kidd on the roof hurls a spray can at my head. I duck, and retrieve it without breaking my stride. I throw it back, hitting the Kidd square in the shoulder.

I'm pleased to see that the Kidds on top of the van look scared and slide to the ground to join the others. What I'm not prepared for is that one or two faces are streaky with tears. The tears almost derail my anger, but then I see the van. The awning droops and there are huge dints in the walls. Spray paint drips over the scarred metal.

'What the fuck are you guys doing?' Lupe's van has

always been off-limits. While almost everything else in Shyness gets tagged and raided, Lupe has always been safe.

There are nine Kidds in total. The strange thing about this group is they all seem the same age, around ten, and no one steps forward as their leader. They haven't moved into fighting formation. It dawns on me that they're not a unit that usually works together. Eventually a snivelling girl in a flannelette shirt speaks up.

'She's a witch,' she says, pointing behind me.

I turn to see Lupe, a smear of colour in the darkness. She's too far away to hear, even though I'm sure she's heard it all before.

'Why do you say that?'

'She cursed us. She cursed all of us.'

Her friends nod their agreement.

'Have you guys been on the post-mix this arvo?' They must be delusional on syrup. I try to imagine Blake in this state, when she was with the Kidds, but I can't. 'Don't give me this curse shit. What's really going on?'

'Look,' says the girl. And she pulls one of the other Kidds forwards. He cradles a still tarsier in his hands. I stifle my surprise at seeing another dead one. It smells ripe, as if it's already been hoarded for a few days.

'It's not asleep,' says the girl, unnecessarily.

'What has this got to do with Lupe?'

She wipes her nose. Her fingernails are ripped and dirty.

'It's not just the furries. All the big Kidds left Orphanville and they wouldn't tell us why. Someone stole all our bikes. There's no food, and the sugar stash is all gone. Building Six caught on fire. No one tells us what to do.'

Lupe has reached us now and stands beside me.

'It's a curse,' says the girl. 'It has to be. And she's what done it.' The Kidds all nod again in unison.

Lupe draws herself up to her full height. She seems to pull power from the shadows surrounding her, becoming clearer and sharper than before. Her accent is thick when she speaks, but her voice is controlled. 'It is not a curse. I am not the person who has done this. But you need to leave now, or I will curse you.'

The Kidds hesitate, unsure whether they're attackers or trying to persuade us of something, or asking for our help. A short Kidd in the unlikely combination of a bike helmet and wetsuit backs away a few steps, but then hesitates, waiting to see if the others are going to follow.

'Maybe you can find out who killed the tarsier, and then you can curse them,' says the flannelette girl in a hopeful voice.

It's all too much for Lupe, who points her finger with the force and conviction of a deity. She hisses a long string of Polish words. 'Leave!'

The Kidds start as if electrocuted, and melt off into the night with eyes as big as satellite dishes.

'What did you say to them?' I'm impressed.

Lupe smiles grimly. 'I tell them they need bath.'

I can see only her back as she steps into her van, but no doubt her smile slips right off her face. She lets fly with another flurry of Polish.

I swear again when I see the inside of the van.

There's broken glass on the floor, pictures hanging askew, books knocked to the ground, a pile of records lying in shards. The fairy lights have been torn down, the remains of the beaded curtain crunch underfoot. It smells suspiciously like a urinal.

I thump the wall with my fist, again and again, until my knuckles ache. 'We shouldn't have let them go. We should make them fix this up.' I try to leave the caravan, fuelled by the buzz of anger, but Lupe stands in my way. For a millisecond I think about pushing her aside, but then good sense kicks in.

Lupe grips me. 'Jethro. Be still now.'

'Why would they think you're to blame?'

'I do not know. I have always fed them, never turned them away. Not like others. But they were full of pain. People do not think clearly in this state.'

'How can you forgive them? Look at this place.'

'What good does angry do?'

Lupe lets my arms go, and pulls several small brown paper bags from her handbag, the takings of her errands.

The bags are printed with an elaborate *W&S*, just like Blake's books.

'First things. I will make tea and I will use your mobile telephone. Then I will clean this shemozzle up. You will help me.'

Lupe takes the packages into the galley kitchen and tosses me a garbage bag. I put everything that's broken beyond repair in the bag and make a pile of things that might be fixed on the table. The gargoyle paperweight I gave Lupe a few years ago for her birthday cowers under the sideboard. One of its horns has broken off.

In the kitchen Lupe murmurs into my phone. When she returns she places a silver tea tray on the table and pours us both cups. She gestures for me to stop cleaning.

'The kitchen is not touched.' She smiles. 'Maybe they still want kebab.'

I squeeze into the bench seat, and sip on the sour-hot liquid. My muscles start to melt. Lupe's tea is working in the usual way.

'Is that what you were doing on Dreamer's Row? Buying tea?'

I always assumed Lupe made her tea herself, but now I realise that doesn't make any sense. There's no room in the van to grow or dry herbs.

'I bought tea from special place, on other side of Shyness.' Lupe looks over her wrecked home without flinching. 'Do you remember your beautiful friend, the wild girl, what she said about this van? She said it was full of crap.'

I smile at the memory. It seems to be getting more difficult to forget Wildgirl the more time passes by. That's the opposite of what's supposed to happen.

'She was right,' Lupe continues. 'It was too busy in here. Time for clearing out.' She puts her cup down and stares at me through the rising steam. 'Tell me again why you do not call her?'

'Lupe, I've told you a dozen times I don't want to talk about this. I don't know why.'

I do know why. Even Lupe doesn't know about the one time I called, and the result.

'You were supposed to battle great evil together.'

'That was just a game, Lupe.'

Except it wasn't. We did battle great evil together, in a way. I only met Doctor Gregory for a few minutes up on that roof, but even in that short amount of time, he managed to say exactly the right things to unsettle me.

'No excuse. I see sparks between you.'

'You sound like you've been talking to Thom. He thinks I need to get laid.'

I regret the words as soon as I say them, but Lupe slaps her knee emphatically. 'Exactly! A young man needs to—'

'Stop!' My face is red. 'Enough. Okay?'

Lupe holds her hands up. 'It's natural, but you don't want to talk about it.'

'I'm less worried about my love life and more concerned about you. What will you do if the Kidds come back?'

The Kidds are desperate enough to act on any stupid suggestion. They seemed to accept that Lupe wasn't to blame, but someone put that idea in their heads in the first place. Someone persuasive. Maybe the same person who's responsible for abandoning them—Doctor Gregory. We realised that night that he set the Kidds up in Orphanville. Gave them bikes, sugar, tarsier. And what he gave he could easily take away. I wouldn't be surprised.

'I thought of this myself. I have called my friend, and I will live at his house.'

'What? Who's that?'

'Janek was the best man at my wedding. He was my husband's best friend.' Lupe leans heavily on the table to get to her feet. She pulls a purple suitcase from a hatch in the floor.

'Oh.' I didn't even know Lupe was married. I never thought to ask, and she never said anything.

'Janek picks me up in his car. I am tired of this van.'

Lupe opens drawers and begins packing a rainbow's worth of dresses into the suitcase.

'How can you leave your home behind?' Panic wells in my chest.

'Time is up for my little caravan kingdom. It's time for a window that does not look onto concrete.'

Lupe hears the betrayal in my voice because she leaves her packing to come over and squeeze my cheeks. How many more things don't I know about Lupe that I never thought to ask? And now she's going away and I won't be able to ask them so easily.

'I'll miss you.' I don't feel ashamed saying this to Lupe. It's the truth. I can't imagine saying it to anyone else but I've told so many truths in Lupe's van it hardly seems to matter.

'Yes, you will,' Lupe says. 'And that is why you will call the wild girl. You need someone.'

'I have Diana and Ortolan,' I reply. Then, because that sounds pathetic, I add, 'And Blake and Thom.'

'Not the same. Ortolan and Diana are your world, but you are not theirs. Same for the others.'

'Gee, thanks Lupe.' I can't keep the hurt out of my voice.

'This is not unkind, this is the truth.' Lupe snaps her suitcase shut.

'I don't need anyone.'

'Not true. You need me and I'm going away.'

Lupe comes over to me at the table. She pulls my head into her stomach and pats my hair. I feel numb. This is what it feels like when people leave. I close my eyes and a memory plays across my lids.

The car is laden to the roof as if we're going on a family camping holiday. My dad slams the car boot, shutting the door on their old life. It's the day my parents left Shyness. The sun has been stuck at half-mast for weeks, but everyone accepts it's only going to get darker. But for now, every day burns with a dim orange haze, like there's a bushfire coming. When the car pulls away, I'm left standing on the front doorstep, watching it go. That night Paul comes over to the house and cooks me dinner, wearing my mum's apron, and talking in a falsetto to cheer me up.

The less I sleep, the less I dream, the more vivid daydreams seem to get.

I flick my eyes open and pull away from Lupe.

'You must promise me that you will call the wild one, and that together you will watch over Paul. I do not trust those blue people.'

'How far away will you be? How will I contact you?'

'Henny Penny,' says Lupe. 'Do you know this story?'

I shake my head. Conversations with her can turn cryptic in the blink of an eye.

'She thinks the sky is falling. Do you see my meaning?'

'Not really.'

'Sometimes you have to let the world end, so you can build a new one.'

I think about the last time Paul and I really laughed together. I get a flash as well of Wildgirl's green-glittered eyelids, and the dead tarsier curled up like a comma on my kitchen bench. Purple in parts of the sky where there should be black. Signs of the world ending.

Lupe pushes me away so she can look at me properly.

'This blackness inside,' she says, thumping my chest. 'You think you are trying to get rid of it, but you hold on more than ever.'

'The sky *is* falling if you're leaving.'

'My boy.' She clutches me close once more, so much that the breath is squeezed out of me. 'I will miss you the most.'

seven

Birds In Winter is dark, except for a faint glow on the first floor. Behind the building the last shreds of a Panwood sunset are scattered low in the sky. Sometimes I like being in other parts of the city at night, to see that they look almost the same as Shyness for at least half of a twenty-four-hour cycle. It makes the way we live seem more normal. But it doesn't work tonight.

I was meant to be here at six-thirty to babysit, but now it's after eight. I insisted on waiting with Lupe until Janek came to pick her up. And then I stayed to board up the caravan and make it secure.

Every instinct tells me to go home or go out all night, run away, but I don't. I turn my key in the lock and drag my feet up the stairs to my execution. The gargoyle I salvaged swings heavily in my jacket pocket.

Ortolan must have heard me come in because she's leaning against her big work table, arms crossed, waiting. I stop once I reach the landing. I see from her face that I was wrong about how pissed off she would be.

'You ruined my night,' she says in a flat voice. She's worse than angry, she's disappointed.

'Yes.' I did ruin her night. Ortolan's wearing an old jumper and slippers but she still has eye make-up on, and her hair is shiny. I look past her to the corner, where Diana's sitting on her bed, jamming her toy giraffe in her mouth. Her eyes are puffy and her nose is running everywhere.

'What's wrong?' It's not like Diana to cry. 'What happened?'

'Nothing.'

'It doesn't look that way.'

I go to walk over to Diana's bed and comfort her, but Ortolan blocks my way.

'It's under control, Jethro.'

'I'm sorry, Flopsy,' I call out. 'We can make pizza another time.'

Diana barely hears me. She's got that blank look she gets when she's up past her bedtime.

'That's not it,' Ortolan says.

'Well, what is it then?'

'It doesn't matter.' Ortolan chews on a strand of hair.

I know it won't mean anything but I say it anyway. 'I'm sorry. I'm sorry. I know I've stuffed up.'

'I hope you've been having fun, whatever it is that you've been doing.'

I could offer an explanation, but I don't. All the words are piled up in my mouth and won't come out. I was so focused on trying to make things right for Lupe, I clean forgot about Ortie and Diana. There must be something wrong with me if I can't keep more than two things in my head at the same time. It's not that difficult.

'There's no point telling you how important tonight was to me'—Ortie's voice wobbles only slightly—'because I don't have the right to ask you to do anything. You don't have to do any of this.'

She's wrong. How can I tell her that I do have to do this, I do want her and Diana to depend on me, after I let her down?

'I don't mind if you don't want to help out, but if you say you are going to do something, then I expect you to do it.' The last sentence has exhausted Ortie. Her shoulders droop inside her oversized jumper. 'You should go home, Jethro.'

Diana is sucking her thumb. She's almost outgrown the habit and only does it when she's really upset.

'Okay,' I say. Looking at Ortie again is not an option. I wait a few seconds to see if I miraculously have something useful to say, but I don't.

I'm halfway down the stairs when Ortolan calls out. 'Are we still on for dinner tomorrow?'

Ortolan doesn't take up much space in the frame of the doorway. Sometimes she doesn't look much older than me, even though there's six years between us. But she's light years ahead of me in knowing how to live properly.

'I have a gig. Is early okay?'

'Early is fine.' Ortolan is unsmiling. 'Go home, Jethro. I know you won't, but I have to say it anyway: go home.'

She's right, I don't go home. The night in my veins keeps me awake, keeps me moving. I'm full of the things I should have said, all the things I couldn't say without feeling like I was making excuses. How can I be sure I won't keep letting her and Diana down? I didn't mean to ruin her night but it didn't stop it from happening.

I cross Grey Street, straight back into Shyness, looking skywards as I walk. The roofs are clear and the lampposts are empty too, so maybe all the tarsier are dying. I think about Ortie standing at the stop of the stairs. This is what I'm scared of. If you don't promise anyone anything then you can't disappoint them. I don't know how many things I can juggle and not fuck up.

I keep walking past my house. It's only a short distance

to the cemetery. The cemetery is one of the few places in Shyness that hasn't been vandalised. Even delinquents have their limits. I never see anyone else here. I don't know why. There's nothing scary about it. It's no darker than anywhere else. In here there are only narrow paths and headstones, tinder-dry pine trees, barely standing, and monuments to the past. There's no life in this place. I'm only scared of the living.

Gram's ashes are stored in a wall, stacked together with the ashes of hundreds of other people. A filing cabinet for the dead. I close my eyes. My other hand goes to my chest, where his lighter rests at the end of a chain. Ortie soldered it for me after I told her how close I came to losing it.

In movies people always crouch by graves and have conversations with their dead loved ones. I don't do that. I cough instead, feeling a howl rise in my throat. I didn't keep trying to call Wildgirl. Thom is too busy for me. Lupe has left. Ortolan is angry. And if Lupe is right, Paul is as lost as I am.

I swallow against the howl, forcing it down, and distract myself by running through my promises to Gram and myself in my head. I'm fooling myself, but the plaque feels warm under my fingers. I promise to take care of Diana, I promise to look out for Ortie, I promise not to make the same mistakes he did. I promise not to let life beat me the way it did him. The whole time I make these promises I wonder if I'll be able to keep them.

The rickety sound of wheels on tarmac jolts me out of my reverie. I follow the sound to the edge of the cemetery, leaning over the low stone fence. A long procession of Kidds travels down the road, maybe fifty of them, with stolen shopping trolleys. The older Kidds push the trolleys and the younger Kidds ride inside, sitting on cardboard boxes holding clothes and toys and games consoles, all their worldly possessions. There are no tarsier to be seen, and the Kidds don't even look at me as they pass, so bleak is their mood. I want to chase after them, but I suddenly feel exhausted. My eyes are sluggish, as if I'm trying to open them under water. I should go home.

I look back into the graveyard. The headstones and obelisks and crypts make an irregular city skyline in miniature. An empty city for the dead, with me the only living person in it. I'm sick of being on my own.

The very act of pulling my phone out of my pocket makes my heart pump so hard I'm surprised Gram's lighter doesn't jump off my chest. My fingers call up her number easily. I've had enough practice.

I let my finger hover above the green call button. This is usually where I chicken out. My finger drops.

The phone rings for a long time with no answer. I'm about to hang up when voicemail clicks on, and the sound of Wildgirl's recorded voice fills my ear.

8

I wake up with a sandpit mouth, in the wedge of sunlight piercing my bedroom window. My skin is hot and baked dry. A book slides off my chest and onto the bed. Urgh. I'm still wearing yesterday's clothes.

'Mum?' I yell out, but I know it's futile. She'll be out on a regular job, cleaning an office building. She gets paid good rates on a weekend.

There are two missed calls and two voicemails on my phone. The first call is from Helen and the other is from an unknown number.

'Nia, darling, just letting you know I've rejigged the rosters so you're only working Saturdays. School starts this week, doesn't it? I've given you the longest shift I can. You can pick up some extra hours in the holidays, okay? And don't forget Shopping Night. Look sharp. You're an *asset to the business*, honey.'

I smile at those last very unHelenlike words. That's one less thing I have to worry about. I'm filled with an unexpected whooshy, sunshine feeling, until the next message starts. The voice is so quiet I have to bring the phone close to my ear.

'Nia...this is Jethro. Please don't hang up. Hear me out...'

There's no danger that I'll hang up. I'm so busy listening to the low rumble of his voice and picturing his blue, blue eyes, that I don't really listen to what he's saying. He talks to the end of the message, cut off by the beep mid-sentence.

Hating myself already, I hit repeat. The whooshy sunshine feeling turns feral. I don't know whether to be pleased or mad.

'...hear me out. I know it's been a long time. There's a lot to tell you. Lupe's left Shyness, that's one thing. It seems like the right time to call. I...I hope you've been well...I'm worried about Paul...'

Okay, make that mad. I choose to be mad. His voice is echoey and whistling, as if he's calling from an open space.

'...I have a gig on tomorrow night. I know it's short

65

notice, but you've never seen us play, and I really want to see you in person to tell you that—'

And this is where the line beeps and cuts him off. Message over.

My bedroom suddenly feels the size of a shoebox. I kick my doona to the floor. Who does he think he is? He ignores me for six months and thirteen days and then calls expecting me to come hear his stupid band? I want to call back and say exactly this. I'd scream except if you scream in the Commons, it's inevitable someone will call the police.

I can't stay here or I'll go crazy.

Plexus teems with the usual Saturday crowds. Normally the influx of tourists annoys me, but today I don't mind getting lost among people. I don't want to spoil the last weekend before school starts with a bad mood. As if I'd call him.

I join the power walkers, sun junkies and pram pushers on the beachside path, where it juts into the sea. The sun still pelts down but the wind carries away its heat. I lean out over the sea wall. My arms get all goosebumpy with the wind's kiss. Ahead of me is the unknowable ocean, stretching further than I can see.

Tomorrow I go back to school and for once the thought doesn't fill me with dread. Things are going well. The universe has hit a delicate balance and I'm trying to keep it that way.

My eyes water from the relentless gust, so I rest my head against my arm. The sea wall is warm against my forehead. Without meaning to, I tune in to the conversation of a group of girls standing a few metres away. It's pretty hard not to listen. They all have high, annoying voices and keep talking over the top of each other.

'Mrs Briggs,' says one girl. 'What a bitch. I can't believe I have her again this year.'

The name catches my attention, and then the voice. I know those voices.

The loudest is Beth Mahoney, but I also recognise Naomi Tran. That means the other two girls must be Ellen and Matilda.

I freeze right where I am, bent over the wall. If they look to their left, they'll see me.

I never found out for sure that they emailed the fake photo of me doing things I've never done to a guy I've never met, to the entire year level. Mum reported it and all four got called separately to speak to the principal, but there was no evidence. I moved schools soon after.

They're going to recognise me any second, and then I don't know what they'll do. Play nice, as if it never happened? Pick up the bitchy comments from where they left off? Part of me used to like the verbal wars, both parties slashing away at each other, with the meanest words we could think of, but I'm not that person anymore.

I get a strange flash of memory, a snippet of Shyness rushing at me. Standing at the top of an Orphanville tower with Wolfboy next to me, looking out at the dark suburb and the starry sky overhead. Feeling as if I had my whole life ahead of me, glittering and mysterious. The opposite of what I'm feeling now.

I straighten up and walk away, expecting my name to be called out at any moment. My legs are shaky. Soon I'm a hundred metres up the path, and when I turn around, the mean girls are coloured specks in the distance.

I cut across the nature reserve to the main road, breathing in exhaust fumes from the cars. The photo was the final way of telling me I didn't fit in at that school, and never would. That everyone else in my year level believed it so easily meant they already thought I was that kind of person anyway. And what had I done to deserve that? Grow up in a rough area? Did being from Plexus Commons automatically mean I was a slut?

But then following that was the night. The night in Shyness that seemed to be the start of everything working itself out. And maybe, if what Ortolan said is true, it was the same for Wolfboy.

He sounded endearingly hesitant in the voicemail. And Lupe leaving is a big deal. She's one of his closest friends.

And he said something about Paul. Paul was nice. I shake my head to clear it. No. No. No.

Cars whiz past me, and a guy leans out of a Valiant and whistles. I hold my head high, pretending I'm on the side of the road in America, or Spain, or Iceland, and I'm about to hitchhike somewhere really cool. You'd be amazed how I can make myself believe my own fantasies. The road wobbles and shimmers ahead.

nine

Diana waits for me at the door of the shop, as if everything is normal. She's covered from head to toe in flapping shreds of colour: mostly red, but with touches of yellow, blue and green. A peaked red hood covers her head. My stomach is jumping. I don't know if Ortolan has really forgiven me for failing to show up on time last night.

'Jet-ro!' Diana hugs my legs, her face turned up to me. 'Where will you live when the moon goes away?'

I pull a face to make her giggle. 'I'll live with you on a boat, Flopsy. We'll be pirates.'

'Silly!' she says approvingly, and drags me up the stairs.

She lets go of my hand and squawks around Ortie's big

work table, flapping her arms up and down. Her cheeks are flushed.

'What are you, Flopsy? Are you a superhero?' But she is already too caught up in her game to answer. She leaps and then flaps, leaps and flaps.

'I'm in here!'

Ortolan hunches over the kitchen bench, wrestling with a tin of tomatoes. The kitchen is full of the smell of onions and olive oil, and clouds of steam. Diana's drawings on the fridge are curling up at the edges. Ortie breaks her cooking to kiss me hello. 'So, I had to quickly sew what you see out there, because today Diana decided she needed to be a bird of paradise. I don't think she's ever seen a tropical bird, but there you go. She'll probably sleep in that tonight. I hope pasta's okay. I didn't have any time to go shopping, so I'm making dinner from whatever's in the cupboard.' She hands me the tin and a can opener. 'Here. This thing has defeated me. Maybe you'll have more luck.'

I'm grateful to have something to do with my hands. The can opener is rusty, but I get it going.

'Good day?' asks Ortolan. Other than talking a million miles an hour, she seems fine.

'Quiet day. I went over some songs for tonight. Blake and I had a funeral in the backyard.' I put the open tin of tomatoes down on the bench.

Ortie throws me a worried look. 'Funeral?'

'I found a dead tarsier and Blake insisted on giving it a proper send-off.'

'You as well?' Ortie peeks into the studio to see if Diana is listening. 'We found one too, behind our rubbish bins. Well, Diana did. That's why she was inconsolable last night.'

'Oh. I thought I'd upset her.'

'No, it was nothing to do with you. She wanted to bury the tarsier in the backyard as well, but I wouldn't let her. I made her put it in the bin.' Ortie tips the tomatoes in the pan. 'Am I a bad mother? I should have let her have her ritual. It's the first time she's seen anything dead, but I didn't want foxes to dig it up again.'

I think of the dog I saw playing with the dead tarsier.

'Nah, you did the right thing.' I watch Diana playing in the studio from the doorway. She's crouched on the floor grooming herself, her cape spread around her like a puddle of tomato sauce. 'She seems fine now.'

'In a way I was relieved she was upset. At least it was a normal response. I wonder sometimes if I'm doing the right thing, raising her so close to Shyness. Half the time she has her head in the clouds. Yesterday she told me she had a conversation with a cat.'

I have to laugh at that. 'She is normal,' I say, even though it's not the best word to describe Diana. 'She's just very creative and imaginative, like you. She'd be like that

72

anywhere. And I'm used to you living so close by.'

'Diana could have started kinder this year, though. Some people are surprised I keep her at home every day. It's hard to explain to them that there's nowhere nearby.'

'Who cares what people say? You're a great mum.' Telling Ortie she's a good mum isn't a substitute for saying sorry. 'I want to apologise again for last night.'

Ortie turns to face me, leaning against the bench. She flaps a tea towel at me. 'You don't have to, Jethro. It's already forgotten.'

I nudge her over so I can reach the stove to stir the sauce. 'I have a surprise for you. So, ah…Blake is going to ride over here in an hour to babysit Diana so you can come to my gig.'

'Really?' Ortolan's face brightens so instantly I know I've done the right thing. I wasn't sure if she'd like me making plans for her. I thought it was worth the risk, though. She doesn't get many nights out.

'I know Blake has never watched Diana on her own before, but I thought it would be all right for an hour or so.'

'It's perfect. That's so thoughtful of you. A few friends were going to pop over for a drink later, so we'll all come.' Ortie fishes a piece of spaghetti out of the pot and bites it. 'Can you get Diana to wash her hands?'

'Sure.'

I turn to fetch Diana from the studio, only to realise

73

she crept into the kitchen while we were talking. She taps her beak against my leg.

'I love Blake!'

Thom is already at the Green Lantern Lounge for sound-check when I arrive. There's zero glamour to the Green Lantern when the lights are up. The black paint on the walls is chipped in too many places to count, the carpet is festering, and the varnish has worn off all the tables.

I shake Vince the sound guy's hand and join Thom on the low stage.

'No Paul yet?' I ask.

Thom looks up. 'Nice to see you too, bro.' He finishes adjusting the mikes and gives Vince a thumbs-up. 'Relax. Paul will show.'

'We haven't rehearsed for two weeks. I've got grounds to be concerned.'

Vince comes over. He wears his jeans so ball-crunchingly tight he has trouble walking in a straight line. 'This equaliser is fucked. I've gotta find the spare desk out back. You can take five.'

'Beers,' says Thom, and jumps down. I follow him to the bar. 'You owe Maggie a drink for letting us use her car.'

'Thanks for picking up the gear from my house.'

He hands me a glass. 'I can't believe Lupe left Shyness,' he says. 'Feels like my childhood is over.'

I snort. 'You've always said she's creepy.'

'She is. All that voodoo shit gives me the heebie-jeebies. But her kebabs were awesome.'

I point at his gut. I don't have to apologise to him for calling him fat the other day. One good thing about Thom is he never holds a grudge. Too much effort involved. 'It's not going to hurt you to eat less kebabs, buddy.'

Thom pats his stomach, rubbing his hand over a lurid floral shirt that smacks of Maggie's influence. There's beer froth around his mouth.

'We can't all be junkyard dogs, Wolfboy. You never get off your arse either, and you still look like you run marathons in your spare time.'

The club is still empty, other than the barman drying glasses behind the bar, and Vince hunched over the sound desk. I drink my beer slowly, deterred by pre-gig stomach jitters.

'Thom, tell me something. That girl Paul was seeing for a while—is that over?'

Thom shakes his head. 'Dude. You are so far behind. Ingrid and Paul broke up a month ago.'

'Right.' Ingrid, that was her name. I never met her but Paul talked about her nonstop for a while there. I'm ashamed I didn't notice they'd broken up. 'Do you think he took it okay?'

'Bro, I don't know. We don't talk about that sort of stuff.

That's your job. If he wanted to talk about it, Paul would go to you.' Thom doesn't seem fazed by that, even though he's known Paul as long as I have. He's so laidback these days he's almost horizontal.

'Were they serious? Should I ask him about it?'

Thom grins. 'I think we should play this show first, before you go into the woods with Paul to play bongos and talk about your feelings. Actually, I think you should forget about the whole thing. If Paul wants to blubber on your manly chest, he'll let you know.'

'There's no chance of that. Paul's been avoiding me. I don't know what I did wrong.'

Thom nudges my arm with his beer. 'Vince is giving you the signal. You're up.'

ten

By ten o'clock I'm cross-eyed with the strain of watching the door. Paul still hasn't arrived, but it's not just him I'm looking out for. My breath catches every time I see a girl who's the right height, or who has long dark hair. But it's never her. Punter after punter drifts in, including Ortolan and her friends, and I should be happy, because there aren't usually this many people for the opening band, but I'm not.

Now that the overhead lights have been turned off the Green Lantern looks halfway passable. The lamps scattered through the club glow with the bare minimum of light to stop people from walking into furniture.

Thom's girlfriend Maggie sits with a table of City

friends who are pretending not to gawp at the ghostniks. Ghostniks are tame by Shyness standards. They dress in all black, like mimes, but with more skulls. Skull earrings, necklaces, hats, tattoos, socks. What I like about ghostniks, and the Green Lantern Lounge, is that the owner always pays us on the night, and that the ghostniks are far too bored and anaemic to throw bottles at our heads. Too cool to clap as well, but I can live with that.

Thom finds me hiding to the side of the stage.

'How much longer do you think we can push it?' I ask.

He shrugs and sips his millionth beer.

'What do we do if he doesn't show?' I ask.

'Play as a two piece?'

It's a terrible idea. There'll be nothing to keep us together without Paul on drums. Vince catches my eye across the room, and raises his eyebrows questioningly.

'Okay,' I say finally. 'If that's what we have to do.'

'Oh. Not necessary.' Thom points to the other side of the room. 'The prodigal son returns.'

Paul skirts the walls like a stray cat. I breathe out in relief. Thom starts plugging in leads.

'Hey, Paul,' I say, as he climbs on stage. 'Cutting it fine, buddy.' He's wearing the same clothes he's been dressed in for months: a threadbare stripy t-shirt and too-short suit pants. His shoulderblades poke out so far underneath his shirt they might be folded wings. Angels don't wear circles as dark as bruises under their eyes, though.

'Jethro. Thom,' he mumbles, and heads straight for his kit.

'See? He's not pissed off at you.' Thom thinks he's speaking softly but I'm sure Paul heard what he just said. I look at Thom's beery face and marvel that he can't see how haunted Paul looks.

I go to the rear of the stage. 'I see the Neural Endings didn't bother to make it for our set,' I say to Paul. I wait for him to make his tired-but-still-funny joke about how the headline band should change their name to the Happy Endings, but he doesn't.

'I'm ready,' he says. He inspects his sticks. Paul has never had a good poker face.

'Everything okay with you?' I ask. I don't expect him to answer me honestly. It's not like we can go into it here in front of all these people.

'Sure,' he says. I catch a glimpse of his eyes before he looks down again.

'Good. We're starting with "Blacklist".'

We barely fit on the cramped stage. I scan the room for the last time. I knew it was a long shot that Wildgirl would come but disappointment still lodges heavily in my stomach. The message I left said none of the things I wanted to say or should have said.

I flip my guitar strap over my head and try to focus.

'We're the Long Blinks,' I mumble into the mike, to resounding silence. Paul counts us in, and we're off. Even though we haven't rehearsed properly for a while we still find each other easily. There's nothing wrong with Paul's rhythm.

Every time we finish a song Ortie whistles through her fingers, and Maggie's table claps. The ghostniks stare and drink wine. We fuck up a newer song but it doesn't seem to matter. Even Paul begins to smile at his kit and nod along. The set races by quickly, until it's time for the last song. We always play this one last.

I take my guitar off and lay it on the amp.

Paul taps out a driving beat and Thom starts up a squalling guitar racket. I grip the mike stand tightly with both hands. This has got to be loose and messy. I sing—

Well, I was low
And you were high
And you said: hey, come on, boy
Let's fly
Well, you were soft
And you felt right
And I said: love you, girl, for just
One night

I know I'm not getting it right. There's no grunt behind

my voice. I try to howl, I really do. To get my voice up on the high note and fill the room, but it doesn't happen. Trying to start the car with a flat battery. The note comes out as a whimper.

I turn away from the audience and come face to face with Paul behind his kit. Strangely, he senses exactly the right thing to do, and shifts the beat down a notch. Thom, after giving us an annoyed look, follows suit, stepping on his pedal and playing a simpler, quieter line.

I repeat the last verse, then hit the chorus again.

Well, we were young
And full of fight
Come and save me now
From these long nights
Dark days
Dark days
Without you, girl
Without you
Dark days

The song's barely over before Thom unplugs his guitar. I want to get off the stage as quickly as I can.

It's left to Paul to say into his mike, 'Thanks, we're the Long Blinks.'

I can't help myself after that. I step back up to the mike.

'Yeah, I want to thank the Happy Endings for inviting us along tonight. You guys rock.'

The ghostniks blink, and drift towards the bar.

'That was different,' Thom says, coiling his leads.

After we've moved our gear off stage I get myself a beer plus one to spare, and join Ortie at her table. Thom sits with Maggie and her group. Paul dances on his own, moving with jerky marionette moves.

'Great show,' Ortie says.

'You don't need to lie on my account. We sucked.'

'No, you didn't. It's been a while since I've seen you play, and you've really improved. I like your new songs.'

I don't agree with her, but I've learned to take compliments and shut up. My beer slides down fast.

One of Ortolan's group, a loud woman with peroxide hair, reaches across me and slaps Ortolan on the arm. 'We don't all have Ortolan's business nous,' she says to the man opposite.

'What do you mean?' asks Ortolan.

'Buying into Panwood while property prices were still low.' The blonde steadies herself by putting her hand on my leg. 'I waited too long and now there's nothing affordable left.'

'It wasn't nous, it was luck,' Ortolan says.

'The market's gone through the roof,' the man says.

I pick the blonde's hand off my leg. Ortolan's fashion

friends can be really annoying. I don't want to join in their stupid conversation but it's reminded me of the darkitect. I lift my glass, toasting myself. Here's to sounding like a bourgeois twat.

'Have you had anyone contact you about buying your place?'

Ortolan's drink straw pops out of her mouth. 'I thought the sun would rise before you showed an interest in real estate, Jethro.'

'No, I saw a man outside your shop the other day. He was checking out your building. I thought someone might have made you an offer.'

'Oh, don't worry about that. That's nothing.' Ortolan sinks into thought, before snapping to attention. 'Look over there.'

Paul hops and spins on the dancefloor, out of sync with the beat as if he's hearing different music from the rest of us. People duck to avoid his flailing arms. A beatific smile is plastered on his face. I'm reminded of Diana flapping and squawking in her bird costume. The ghost-niks point and smirk and whisper. I can't decide if it's sad or admirable that Paul doesn't care what people think of him.

'What's wrong with him?' Ortolan asks.

'Lupe asked the same thing. Thom thinks I'm imagining what a loose unit he is these days. All we can figure out is that he broke up with his girlfriend and he's cut up about it.'

Ortolan watches Paul in frowning silence for a minute before speaking. 'You know, this is exactly what worries me about Shyness.'

'Bad dancing?' I try to lift the mood. Ortie doesn't fall for it.

'I've never told you this, but Paul kept in touch with me for years when no one else did.'

'I sort of knew that,' I say.

'Even when I was overseas. But he hasn't even said hello to me tonight. I waved earlier and he looked at me like he doesn't remember who I am. I can't help thinking that the Darkness wears everyone down gradually. I don't want that for Diana.'

'Paul's a completely different person to Diana.'

'Maybe when she's his age that's exactly what she'll be like.' Ortolan points. 'Is that the Paul you know?'

It's not. Is this what Lupe was warning me about, the Darkness getting inside people? Thom may be pissed off that I can't howl, but Ortie is probably pleased.

'What if it's the other way around?' I reply, forming the idea as I talk. In my peripheral vision I see the Neural Endings moving onto the stage. 'What if it's the bad stuff inside people that makes the Darkness? What if we're the cause, not the result?'

'I don't know.' Ortolan gnaws on the flattened end of her straw. 'Either way, life is much better if you don't let yourself give up totally, even when bad things happen. You need to find a balance between acknowledging what's passed and getting on with your life. It's hard but you have to at least try.'

I know she's thinking of Gram when she says this. A lesser person would have fallen apart when he died, but Ortolan seems forged in fire. I'm trying to formulate a response when she half-rises from her chair. Paul has fallen to the ground. He kicks his legs dead-bug style. Horizontal and still dancing.

'Shit.'

I make my way as quick as I can to the space that's opened up around him. When I lean over him he's grinning as if he's having the time of his life. He shakes me off as soon as he's standing again.

'Don't worry, don't worry.' He squints at me. Bleary eyes, feverish skin. He was fine when we were playing, so how did he get messed up so fast?

'Let's sit down for a while, buddy. You want some water?'

Paul looks off into the far corners of the ceiling. 'How come you always know when you're awake, Jethro? How do you do that?'

'What?'

He rips away from me, into the thickening crowd. I let

him go. I force myself to turn my back on him. I can't talk to him when he's in this state.

When I make it to their table Thom has his arm around Maggie and holds her City friends in thrall. He's telling them about the time the Kidds tried to roll him for his biker jacket, and how he fought them off with his bare hands. He doesn't mention that the Kidds were all under ten, and that this happened two years ago. Somehow he manages to jam the car keys in my shirt pocket without missing a beat in his story. I grab an amp and head for the door.

Maggie's blue hatchback is the only car parked on the street. The pole of the no-standing sign next to it is weirdly shaped. Someone has strapped tin cans to it, using the plastic wrist ties you get at music festivals.

The cans are filled with dirt and plants are growing in them. They're flowers, I suppose, but they're the strangest flowers I've ever seen. Jet black, with three large petals. Small black flower heads in the centre, and long whiskers that trail over the edges and down the pole. Aliens or monsters as much as plants. I take a photo of them with my phone.

When all the gear's loaded I take the keys to Thom. Paul is near the stage, thrashing about to Neural Endings, a band he's only had bad things to say about in the past. They've built a clashing wall of sound that makes my brain hurt. The ghostniks have shaken off their listlessness and collide in the mosh. The beer has loosened my tongue.

Made all my thoughts want to float out my mouth. I'm pushing through the crowd to Paul when I see a guy in a pale blue shirt moving in the same direction.

Paul sees him coming and tries to force his way out of the crowd. Blue shirt closes in, but Paul pushes him away and shakes his head. Go away. When the guy tries to hand him something, Paul practically elbows people in the face to get away.

I follow the blue shirt onto the street and tap him on the shoulder. He jumps and cowers, as startled as a rabbit.

'Sorry, sorry.' I make my voice light and friendly. 'I'm not following you, but I'm a good friend of Paul's. He's had a few tonight, hey? Was there something you needed to give him?'

The man is nervous, quivering slightly behind silver glasses. From the neck up he's desperate to run away, from the neck down he's stuck to the ground.

'This.' The man shoves a card into my hand. 'I'll be in trouble if he doesn't get it.'

'Sure.' I look down at the piece of cardboard. Pale blue and printed with writing on one side. The words are blurry.

The man ducks his head, and turns to leave.

'Hey, I've been wondering, what's slippage?' I ask.

He turns back towards me, his face a white, lopsided blob. 'Oh no, you're real. You're definitely real,' he says.

11

My hands shake so much I can't put my eyeliner on straight. I wipe it off and try again.

'Nia, are you sure you don't want any of this takeaway?'

Mum peers in. She's just got back from her evening class. I blink my eyes, Bollywood-heavy with eyeliner and mascara, and shake my head at her reflection. Even thinking about food makes me queasy.

'I'm not hungry.'

'You've got to eat, baby.'

She comes in and squeezes my waist. I doubt she cares if I eat dinner or not, it's just this routine we have to go through. I look at our faces side by side in the mirror. She looks tired but happy. I never used to like it when people said we looked alike, even worse when they said we looked like sisters, but now I have to admit even I can see the resemblance. We both have the same round cheeks and stubborn mouths.

'You're all gussied up. Where are you going again?'

I sigh. Sometimes I hate this new policy we have about telling each other the truth. 'I'm meeting a boy.'

'Does he have a name?'

'Uh, Jethro.'

'Oh, good.' Mum does another button up on my shirt. 'I thought you were going to say that teen-wolf boy from Shytown.'

'Mum, that was ages ago.' I pretend to fix my hair in the mirror. My voice is too-bright and fake. 'And it's Shyness, not Shytown.'

'I know it was ages ago, but I don't forget boys who sound like bad news, Nia.'

'You never met him.'

'I didn't have to meet him; you stayed out all night with him. When I was your age I had the same lack of taste.'

'Oh, I bet Fish Creek was just *swimming* with bad boys.'

'Don't joke, Nia. It landed me in a whole lot of trouble.'

'Fortunately, you've raised a very sensible, mature young woman with extremely excellent taste.' I undo the top button of my shirt again, and push my ladies up. Better.

'I don't doubt it, honey.' Mum backs towards the door. 'You look hot by the way.'

I throw a shower-puff at her. 'Don't say "hot" to your own daughter, Mum, that's just plain weird. I'm going to impress him with my giant brain.'

She smiles and leaves me alone. I close the bathroom door and jam a towel in the gap. God, why did she have to do that? I was all ready to be honest with her, why does she have to make it so hard?

I pull my phone out, wondering even as I'm finding his name in my address book whether this is the action of a dignified human being.

I am meeting Wolfboy; he just doesn't know it yet.

The phone barely rings once before he answers. I watch myself in the mirror, tilting my head and imagining I'm a sassy actress in a black and white movie.

'Nia, is that you?' His eager voice almost unhinges me. 'How are you?'

'Do you want to meet at the Diabetic in an hour?' I close my eyes and screw up my face while I wait for him to answer.

'Yeah, yeah, sure, of course.' He sounds surprised but doesn't hesitate. 'But…are you sure you don't want to meet somewhere else? The Diabetic isn't the nicest place.'

'Nup, it's non-negotiable. Meet me there in exactly an hour.'

He begins to protest, but I hang up. He needs to know we're doing this my way, or not at all.

My heart is galloping. There were so many mysteries after that night, not least why he never called. The thought that I might be about to find out some of what happened freaks me out.

At least he said yes. He said yes.

I put on Mum's best red lipstick and then message Ruth to tell her I won't need her to be my Plan B for the evening. She replies straightaway: *Good. On the couch with a packet of Tim-Tams and Casablanca. What are you wearing?*

I look down at my black jeans and tight patterned shirt. I could have gone for my boots with the low heels, but I decided on trainers instead. You never know who—or what—you might have to run from in Shyness.

I message her back: *Glamour up top, girl next door below.* My phone beeps seconds later: *That's the way! Good luck x.*

Mum and our next-door neighbour Stella are sitting on the couch, watching telly and hoeing into tubs of noodles. There's an open bottle of chardy on the coffee table, and Stella's already listing to the side. She's eighty, so it doesn't take much.

'All right, see ya!'

'Got your phone?' Mum asks.

'Yep.' I'm desperate to leave without a fuss, but my eye is caught by something on the kitchen bench.

'Doesn't school start tomorrow?'

'Yes.' I walk over to have a look.

'Not too late then. Eleven.'

'Stop showing off in front of Stella.' I slam my hand down. There are two train tickets on the bench, fanned out for me to see. Leaving on Wednesday afternoon. *Two* tickets.

Mum turns her head. 'It's a school night, Nia. Eleven.'

'Okay.' I force myself over to the door. Now is not the time to pick a fight about going with Mum to the country.

'Nia…'

I grit my teeth. 'Yeeees?'

'Have fun, honey.'

Stella whistles pervily, and I race to get away before I start shooting my mouth off.

By the time I've caught the two trains that get me to Panwood train station and walked down O'Neira Street, seeing the street more and more abandoned and the buildings get crappier and crappier, I think I might throw up from nerves. I stride into the night with equal amounts of fizz and dread in my step. The quiet here is unsettling. No distant buzz of cars, or clatter from televisions or parties or dinners. No rustling in the trees. The dark looks the same as regular City dark, but I can feel the difference.

I shouldn't have worn a shirt this colourful. People in Shyness are fans of black-on-black, and for good reason.

It helps them disappear in the night, so they don't get harassed by monkeys, or Kidds, or slimy evil doctors in fancy cars. I spot the roof of the Diabetic Hotel again in the distance.

I'm so intent on getting there that I don't pay much attention to the whine at first. When it sounds again, I stop, every part of me alert. I'm being watched.

I force my frozen hands to get my phone out of my bag and raise it to my ear, ready to hold a loud conversation with an imaginary friend. I hear the noise again. A squeaking sound, like a gate with rusty hinges blowing in the breeze. There's no wind tonight.

Next to me, a narrow wedge of park lies in the shadows of surrounding buildings. The silhouettes of a slide, a climbing frame, a seesaw and a roundabout crowd the centre.

I take a few halting steps towards the playground.

I don't know why. I should be running in the other direction.

The park isn't empty. Against the predictable straight edges of the play equipment there's something else. Someone is in the park. My heart goes thumpety-thump.

The metal roundabout moves idly, whining as it turns. Wolfboy spins to face me. He plants his feet on the grass and the roundabout comes to a halt.

'Ready or not, here I come,' he says.

He smiles up at me. Flashing white teeth, eyes so obviously blue, even in this darkness. There are curls over his collar; his hair has grown. I'm filled with a rush of unexpected pleasure to see him. Whatever fantasy I had in my head of what Wolfboy looks like, it's now clear I haven't been fantasising hard enough, not nearly.

'Hi, you,' I say, and expect my sentence to continue after that, but it doesn't. I dig the toes of my sneaker into the tanbark. I suddenly remember to drop my phone hand away from my ear.

'It's been too long,' he says. 'Nia.'

I'm full of uncertainty. He looks more like a man than I remember. I feel our age difference keenly.

'You were supposed to meet me at the Diabetic,' I cross my arms over my chest, determined to stick to the script.

'I knew you'd come this way. I didn't want you to walk too far on your own.'

'I can take care of myself.' I think I said something similar to him the night we met. The difference now is that I know more about Shyness. It occurs to me that it would have been a good idea to bring something to defend myself with, but what? There's literally zero weaponage in our apartment. I don't think an eyelash curler would do.

'I've no doubt about that.'

Wolfboy stands and moves out of the shadows. I crane my neck. I'd forgotten how tall he is. He leans down to kiss me hello and I twist my head to the side. A fleeting sense of fear surprises me. Any illusion I'd had that he was like any of the other boys I know is drifting away in the night.

He stands there, head to the side, smiling at me with what seems like genuine pleasure, but all I can see is the power hiding in his body. I blink and get a flash of that night: Wolfboy sprinting between the towers of Orphanville, gliding so fast I couldn't see his arms and legs move.

I forgot he wasn't a normal boy. I don't even know where his power begins and ends. I move away from him.

'Come on then,' I say.

If Wolfboy looks better than I remember, then the inside of the Diabetic Hotel looks worse, much worse. The lime-green walls are sicklier, the tables stickier and the carpet smellier. Apart from a heavily tattooed guy hitting the cigarette machine, we're the only customers. Maybe the pub was always this crappy and I was starry-eyed about it.

The barman brings us beer without asking, and once again I'm forced to pretend I like the stuff.

'Déjà vu,' says Wolfboy, looking at me then down at the counter. 'You know, no one comes here anymore. There was a big brawl here the night we met, and a guy got stabbed.'

'I'm a hopeless nostalgic,' I say. I'm painfully aware of how close Wolfboy is, on the stool next to mine. I wish we were sitting at a table; then I could look at him without tilting my head awkwardly. I sip my beer, a polite pretend sip. He doesn't respond.

The seconds tick by. I thought when we were standing there in the dark playground and I saw him smile that things were going to be all right between us, but what did I think would happen tonight? We barely know each other, and we haven't talked for six months.

I catch the barman's eye and I can tell he sees me drowning. I should be thankful there's hardly anyone else here to witness my humiliation.

'Thanks for calling,' Wolfboy says eventually. He drums his fingers against the counter.

I draw swirls on my sweating beer glass. There's a big fat elephant sitting in this room, perched on a stool next to us, drinking rum and coke. I want Wolfboy to tell me why he didn't call for so long, and then I want him to tell me why he's calling me now. And I don't want to have to ask because I don't want him to think I care.

'You're not drinking,' says Wolfboy.

'Neither are you.' My hands are trembling. I sit on them.

'I'm hung-over.' He looks at me sideways. 'A girl stood me up last night so I drank too much. I was really bummed out.'

'Oh yeah?' I stare back. 'That's nothing. This guy said he'd call me, and he never did.'

'Nia,' Wolfboy says, going all soft around the eyes. He touches my arm and I freeze. It would be easier to lean into him than to make conversation. There's a magnetic pull there, a promise. I can't pretend there's not. There are too many memories of that night to keep at bay.

I pick up my glass as an excuse to shake off his hand. The freezing mouthful of liquid is as cold as the anger that has me unexpectedly in its grip.

'What's going on with Paul?' I feel close to panic. I should never have come here.

'We don't have to talk about that.'

'You obviously wanted to talk to me about it, so why are you being so coy?'

Wolfboy shrugs and pulls something from his jacket pocket. He slides it along the counter, daring to look at me. I got spooked too easily in the park. Even though his hair is longer and wilder, he seems less wolfish than when we met. Only the faintest of stubble dusts his cheeks. I look down.

A postcard. Plain blue, with a small drawing of two flowers above the words: DATURA INSTITUTE. I turn it over and it says 'You are due for a visit' in elegant dark blue writing. There's an address in the bottom corner. My stomach is sliding so fast it will be crashing through the basement in seconds.

'What's this?'

'I think Paul is mixed up with these people.'

I flip the card back to the flower side. 'What do they do? Ikebana?'

'I don't know.'

'Why are you worried? It could be harmless.'

I met Paul that night, and he seemed like a really great guy. The sort of friend you could depend on, unlike Wolfboy's el sleazo friend Thom.

'It's hard to explain.'

I turn sharply in my seat to look at him. 'Well, you'd better try. Because I caught two trains here in the dark, and school starts tomorrow.'

Wolfboy winces and I think I shouldn't have mentioned school.

'Paul's been acting weird since he broke up with his girlfriend. He goes off for days at a time. Lupe spotted him hanging out with these Datura people, and then one of them gave me that card. It's too much of a coincidence that he started acting distant right around the time he's seen with them. I know Paul. And he's not himself at the moment. He was really out of it last night.'

It's an uncharacteristic flood of words, coming from Wolfboy. The truth is out. This is why he called me after so many months. Not when he wants me, but when he needs me for something. He really did just want to see me so he could workshop another one of his Shyness dramas.

When I speak my voice is strained. 'So you want me

to come with you and break into this Datura place and liberate, I don't know, all the poor flowers held prisoner there, and find out exactly what's going on with Paul, even though, I don't know, it might be easier to ask him yourself?'

'No, of course not. I was just happy you called. I don't need you to do anything.'

Wolfboy looks so bewildered I can't believe he's really that thick. I slip off my stool. I want to accelerate until the end of this whole painful scenario and I can go home.

'I don't have much time, so let's go.'

'What…Nia…'

'You want to stay here?' I point at the tattooed guy, who's stopped beating up on the cigarette machine and is crooning along to the jukebox using a pool cue as a microphone. 'Maybe you can hook up with that guy. He looks like he needs someone to hold him tonight.'

'No,' says Wolfboy. 'I want to be wherever you are.'

twelve

The Datura Institute is easy enough to find, a short walk away at the end of Oleander Crescent. We stroll past it several times, keeping to the far footpath, before I drag Nia up the driveway and onto the porch of the house opposite. She resists the pull of my arm.

'How do you know someone doesn't still live here?'

'Blank windows. Can't smell any food cooking.' I point at the garage, which is empty with the roller door up. 'Car's gone. Power lines cut.'

There's an old-fashioned swing-seat on the porch, attached to the roof with chains. I try it out and it seems safe.

'I can't see properly,' says Nia, trying to shuffle forwards on the seat, only to be shunted back on every down swing. 'Quit making it swing.'

I'd find her irritation funny, if it was only about the chair. But it's not. When she called I thought I'd been given a second chance. Now I can see it's not going to be so easy. I don't know what I can say to make her relax. I didn't expect to be sitting in the dark outside the Datura Institute. My hand goes up to the lighter. Maybe danger doesn't follow me. Maybe Nia chases it like a dog chases cars.

'There's nothing to see anyway. Just the fence.'

Everything on the street is still. No wind, no sound. It's as if the earth itself has stopped breathing.

The Datura Institute looks like an original old-money property, perched on the hill. It's hidden behind a fortress-like brick wall as tall as the towering eucalypts that used to line this street. There's a single barred gate that shows a narrow path to the front door. The glimpse we got through the gate was of a grand two-storey building with lots of windows.

I look at Nia. I can't think of her as Wildgirl now that she's in front of me. That name belongs to that first night. She looks straight ahead, hands braced on her knees and feet pushed into the floor in case I try to make the seat swing again. Her black hair falls about her face and shoulders. Lips blood red. Eyelashes swooping. It's unfortunate that the more annoyed she gets, the prettier she looks. I've

101

thought about sitting next to her again, like this, alone and in the dark, more times than I can count. We would talk in my version, though.

'Did you get grounded after that night?'

She answers without looking at me. 'No. Mum was surprisingly cool about it. She knows...she knows I met someone, but I let her think that Rosie and Neil stayed with us all night, that we hung out as a group.'

'Oh, Neil,' I say, remembering her boss greasing me off at the Diabetic right before I ran off with his favourite employee. 'How is Neil?'

The corner of Wildgirl's mouth twitches. 'No idea. I quit that job. I work at a vintage store now.' She finally turns to me. 'Actually, it's a funny thing. Ortolan came into my work this week.'

'Ortolan?' She didn't say anything about seeing Nia.

'Yeah. Apparently she comes in every few months.'

'Did you talk to her?'

'A little bit.'

'Oh.' I mull this over. I thought Nia and my worlds were separate. I had no idea Ortolan made so many forays into other parts of the city. 'Is that why you called me tonight?'

Nia doesn't answer.

'I babysit Ortolan's daughter Diana all the time. She's a great kid. You should meet her.'

Nia nods, but not very enthusiastically, and I'm an idiot

for suggesting it. Ortolan and Diana are probably like TV characters to her. People and lives she heard about once upon a time and then forgot about. She looks towards the Datura Institute. I realise then that she's bored. First I piss her off at the pub, and then we come here and I bore her.

'Things have changed,' I say, lamely.

'For me too,' she replies, but something across the road is taking the greater part of her attention. She's getting away from me. 'Wolfboy. Look.'

There are two people walking towards the institute, a man dressed in blue, and a younger boy wearing all black. I watch the man closely. It's not the same guy as last night.

'See the guy in blue? That's what some of them wear. It's a uniform.'

The boy drags his feet, his arms hanging limply by his side. They reach the front gate. The man looks left to right quickly before turning the gate handle. The gate is unlocked.

'That other one wasn't Paul, was it?' Nia asks.

I shake my head.

'Are they Dreamers?' Nia asks. 'The way the younger guy was walking was a bit Dreamer-ish.'

'No.' But then I remember the woman on Dreamer's Row. She may have been dressed in blue, but she definitely lived in that house.

'Well, at least now we know regular people can go in.'

There's something in Nia's tone that sends alarm bells ringing. That and the exaggerated innocence on her face.

'No way.'

'Try and stop me,' she says. Before I can react she stands and pushes down on the edge of the seat, hard. I hold onto it as it rocks violently. It's so unexpected that it takes me longer than it should to get gravity under control. Dust flies up in a cloud off the seat and porch floor. To add insult to injury I start sneezing.

Once I've righted myself I run to the end of the driveway and crouch behind the letterbox. Oleander Crescent is deserted again in both directions, and the fence of the Datura Institute is a faceless wall. The gate is closed. No sign of her anywhere. I slam my fists down into the dirt and swear quietly. Fuck. I let her disappear into thin air.

I bow my forehead all the way down to the dirt and try to think. Do I cross the road and go through the gate? Would she really go in there? Or is she hiding around the corner to taunt me?

Damp soaks through my jeans at the knees. I count slowly to ten. A foot digs under my shoulder, pushes me upwards. I sit up. She stands calmly in front of me. Not even out of breath.

'You praying or something?' she says.

I'm up in a flash, and pulling her by the arm, down Oleander towards O'Neira Street.

'Ouch!' she protests. 'You're hurting my arm.'

I let her go, but I keep walking fast, forcing her to trot to keep up. I breathe down the red wave that threatens to engulf me. It laps over me then flows away.

'Don't you want to know what was inside the fence?'

'No,' I say. 'Sorry. Your arm. Sorry.'

'I'll tell you anyway.' She walks ahead of me, backwards, talking as fast as she can. 'I go through the gate and I can't see anything. So I stick to the path. There's a light on in the house. I don't know if it was an automatic thing because those guys just went through, but it was enough to see the sign next to the door. Plaque actually, gold plaque. It said: The Datura Institute—no surprise there. Then under that, *Doctor Gregory*, with a whole bunch of letters after his name.'

I stop.

'Oh, come on,' Nia says. 'Don't tell me you're surprised? This has Doctor Gregory's fingerprints all over it. From the moment you told me I knew it had to have something to do with him. And I'm not even from around here.'

'You must be smarter than me then,' I say. 'Did anyone see you?'

'No.'

'There could be cameras.'

'I didn't see any.' A long pause while she searches my face. 'Aren't you going to thank me?'

'No. I'm going to get you home on time.' I start walking again, slower this time. Why would Paul let himself have anything to do with Doctor Gregory? I told him more about that night on the roof than I told anyone else. He knows the things that Doctor Gregory said to try to manipulate me.

I sense Wildgirl looking at me, but I ignore her. We walk in silence, over the border to Panwood. I barely register the moment we cross. Up ahead there are traffic lights and cars and the station.

'You don't have to walk me all the way.'

'It's no problem.'

The station glows orange in the night. There are people waiting on the platforms, and the ticket office is open. There are still a few minutes before the train is due.

We stop in front of a circular flowerbed.

'I'll leave you here then,' I say to my toes.

'Why didn't you call me?'

A breeze blows Nia's hair about. She looks beautiful and golden and unknowable. Her shirt is scattered with tiny coloured stars, mirroring the sky above.

'I did.'

'I don't mean after six months. Why didn't you call me after that night?'

'I did call you. A week later.'

'You're such a liar.' She marches up the path towards

the ticket gates. I chase after her, stopping her, careful not to grab her arm as tightly as before.

'Nia, I did call you. Your mum answered and I asked to speak to you, and she said—well, she just—she said no.'

'What?' Her eyes are wide and incredulous.

'I thought maybe you asked her to say that. I wanted to speak to you, but I wasn't going to push it.'

The station lights starburst behind her. 'I don't believe you. Number one, my mum wouldn't do that. She never told me anything about a phone call from you. Number two, say on the off chance that she did do that, why didn't you keep trying? You could have called me again.'

I don't have any answers. She stands her ground, making it clear she expects something. I open and close my mouth.

'I'm talking to you now,' I mumble eventually. 'Lupe said I should call you, and—'

'Wait. Wait!' She holds up her hand. She's crackling and sparking like pine cones in a campfire. 'You called me because *Lupe* told you to?'

I'm tricked into nodding.

'Wow.' She goes very still. 'I am really stupid. To think that you called for any other reason.'

'But you called me tonight! You made me talk about Paul. You wanted to go to the Datura Institute. You snuck in through the gate. You like this espionage stuff.'

It's the same as it was that first night. Wildgirl playing in the dark suburb, shaking things up like we're in a giant snow dome, and then going back to her normal life. Leaving me in a blinding storm, not knowing which way's up.

'You called me tonight,' I repeat. 'Do you want to mess up my life?'

Nia is speechless. Her red mouth shocked open. Tears well in her eyes, but she blinks them away.

'You don't know what you want, Jethro,' she says. 'Your life is already messed up. You don't need me to do that for you.'

If I could retrieve my words I would, grab them out of the sky and hide them where they can't be seen. The crossing bells start to ring, the boom gates lower, and Nia turns and runs for the platform.

thirteen

I stand at the crossroads, at the corner of Grey and O'Neira. I'm flooded with so much static I don't know what to do with it. My hands curl by my side, my neck forces my head back. The night stops.

In a swift flash I gather the black sky from above and pull it down into my gut, swallowing it whole. It cuts deep inside and then it's rising, burning a stinging path up my windpipe.

I scream. I howl.

The sound reverberates inside my head, bounces and multiplies. I try to shake it off, make it stop.

I choke, I scream, I howl.

I'm bent over, hands on knees, close to vomiting. My

heart pounds but I'm finally quiet. A few people stand on the stairs of the Diabetic, faceless plastic figurines. One raises an arm and points. I thought I was done with this.

I stumble over to a wall and lean against it until I get my breath back. I'm still puffing when my phone rings. For one deluded second, I think it's Wildgirl calling me from the train, but it's not.

'Ortolan?' I try to sound normal. 'How's it going?'

'Jethro, are you all right?'

I swallow. 'I'm glad you called. Can I come over?'

'I thought long and hard about whether I should tell you I saw Wildgirl.' Ortolan positions the heater to blow on her slippered feet. We sit downstairs, in the dark and empty shop, so we don't wake Diana.

'I decided not to tell you before you played. I'm sorry. I should have made sure I told you afterwards.'

'It's okay,' I say. 'It wouldn't have made a difference. I think she hates me.'

'I'm sure that's not true.' Ortie stirs sugar into the tea and hands me the cup. 'From what you've told me she'd be angriest at her mum.'

'Her mum was probably right. It's best for Nia if I stay away from her.'

'With all due respect, Jethro, I think that's bullshit.'

I accidentally swallow a mouthful of scalding tea. Ortie hardly ever swears.

'If Nia's mother actually met you, then she'd quickly realise what I already know. You're polite and sensitive, and you always try to do the right thing by people. And according to my friend Kara—you remember the blonde woman from last night?—you wear a pair of jeans very well.'

I scald my mouth again. 'You better watch it,' I say, trying to deflect my embarrassment. 'I'll get a big head.'

'Not a chance.'

Ortie reaches out and absentmindedly fiddles with a dress hem. 'I sort of understand where her mum is coming from. I lie to Diana sometimes if she needs protecting from a certain truth. I'm not excusing what she did—it was misguided—but I do understand that...*tigress* feeling.'

'It's done now,' I say. 'Everything is fucked.'

'I think you can still save it.'

'Maybe,' I say. 'I've got other things to worry about.' I stare at the phalanx of draped mannequins guarding the front window.

'You mean Paul?' asks Ortolan, and I nod, but I don't tell her about Doctor Gregory and the blue people.

'I don't want to add to your worries, Jethro,' Ortolan hesitates. 'But I need to talk to you about Blake.'

'Oh no,' I say. 'What happened?'

Already I'm thinking of possibilities: Diana cutting up her bedspread, or filling the bath with tinned spaghetti, or running a flying fox from the first-floor window. All things she's tried to get me to agree to in the past.

'Diana said that Blake took her out of the house last night.'

'No,' I say straightaway. 'Blake wouldn't do that.'

'That's what my first thought was. But Diana said very clearly, several times when I asked her, that Blake took her to see the Queen of the Night.'

'The Queen of the Night? What's that? Is it a movie?'

'No, Diana said it's a person.' Ortie sighs. 'I know, it sounds like a game or something made-up. When I asked Diana if she meant a real or pretend person, she said real. Not that that means anything.'

'It's not like her to lie to you, though. She tells you everything.'

'That's true. She also tells me she had a tea party with the moon.'

'I'm so sorry, Ortie. I thought Blake could be trusted.'

'It's not your fault. But can you ask Blake about it? I'll feel better if I know exactly what happened.' Ortolan goes to the lacquered desk in the far corner.

'Here.' She hands me a piece of ribbon. I take it, confused. 'I think this is going to help you solve a few things.'

Blake isn't in her bedroom when I get home, so I double back to Paul's room at the front of the house. The room is unsurprisingly empty and stale. Paul still hasn't been home. No satchel. I check under the blow-up camping mattress. Nothing. I'm not sure what I'm looking for anyway. My throat still feels raw.

I message Thom to see if Paul crashed at the cottage last night, but he could be behind the brick walls of the Datura Institute for all I know. I can't believe this has been happening right under my nose.

There's an inner tube in the far corner, and a messy stack of papers being held down by a tin of baked beans: a stash of flyers, some for our gigs, some for other bands, black market sales, and a two-month-old ticket for a party at the old municipal pool. Nothing with the Datura Institute logo on it. Then I see Paul's spidery handwriting on the back of the pool party ticket.

Velodrome

Sunday, darkest night

I stare at it. There's only one velodrome in Shyness. It's close to my old high school. As far as I know the cycling track and club has been abandoned for years. Although I probably wouldn't know if something was there. The last time I was close by was that night with Nia, on our way to Orphanville. We were stopped by three Kidds dressed as pirates.

And one of them did say something about the velodrome.

I strain to remember the pirate captain's exact words.

She said: *As soon as I saw you I thought you were off to the velo. The bike place. The dog place.*

I've underestimated how eerie the walk to the velodrome is going to be. As soon as I cross the misty creek I regret not riding. The creek and the corridor of parkland have changed in six months. More dead trees have toppled, the undergrowth has rotted flat, trying to meld with the ground.

My mind can't settle: Paul, Nia, Paul, Nia. He's been lying to me. He's caught up in something to do with Doctor Gregory. She's gone.

I should have said something different to her at the station. I should have told her that I can't believe I ever got to kiss her. But I didn't say anything right. And now she'll find some other guy. She'll change her mind, because that's what people do. They change their minds, they don't call. They wait a few days so they don't look too keen. When there's an obstacle they give up too easily. They wonder why someone would ever be interested in them. The memories that once seemed so certain fade and become more like fantasies or dreams.

Ahead lie the dark buildings of Orphanville. The night is cloudy, with no illumination from the moon, and the towers are darker than I've ever seen them.

The velodrome is further away than I thought.

I pass the bridge where we met the three pirates and I run until the towers pass silently. I finally spot a smudge of light in the distance. As I draw closer to the velodrome, my eyes sharpen and my ears sharpen; everything moves into clear focus.

The velodrome fits into the basin of a man-made hill the shape of a small volcano. Light bleeds from the lip. Something, some sense or instinct, prickles the back of my neck. I reach the top of the hill and look down. Two trucks are parked near the centre of the bowl, with floodlights running off their batteries. The lights are focused on a huge cage. When I see what's inside, I understand why the pirate called this the dog place.

fourteen

There are about forty people in the velodrome, most of them gathered around the cage, cheering and yelling. Their excitement is palpable. Off to the side is a set of decrepit bleachers with a handful of people lingering on the steps.

I pass two Locals scuffling in the dust. One has the other on the ground in a headlock. He sees me, and pauses to give me a grin and a thumbs-up.

The cage is a big cube, about twice my height. I grab onto the wire and press my face close. My nostrils flood with the scent of sweat and adrenaline.

There are two men fighting inside, throwing themselves wildly at each other. And now that I'm closer I can see I wasn't wrong. They're people like me. Once or twice I've glimpsed others around Shyness, but not for a while. The sight used to scare me. Now I'm interested.

The taller man wears only a tatty pair of shorts. His body is covered with hair so dense it should really be called fur. Bare feet dancing, he circles the other guy with his fists up near his face. I watch his eyes, and it gives me a shiver. He's taller than me, heftier, and more animal. Recent howl aside, I am not this guy. I couldn't become this guy.

The other fighter looks more regular. An athletic guy in a tracksuit, except for the fact that his fingers end in sharp, curving claws, and his shaved head is tattooed all over with blue lines. He swipes with a lightning paw. The tall man falls to the dirt, clutching his shoulder, and the small crowd explodes into cheers. My fingers twitch at my side.

An umpire lying face-down on the wire roof above the fighters counts down as the clawed guy pins the other down. The umpire calls it, and the clawed guy leaps to his feet, arms held up victory. The tall man rolls over and spits blood onto the dust.

The guy standing next to me swears, rips up a piece of paper and stamps on it. He catches me staring.

'Fifty bucks, down the drain.'

Next to the cage, standing on a tall lifesaver's chair, an old man in a gaudy checked suit calls into a megaphone.

'Victory to Talon! Next up, Pussycat Battle!'

The men clear out of the cage, and two more fighters enter. I blink. They're girls like none I've ever seen.

One is short and wiry, with two black buns on either side of her head. She wears tight black leather, trailing a tail behind her. I try to see where the tail joins her body, but she weaves restlessly, making it difficult. Her skin is slick with sweat or oil.

The other girl-fighter is taller, more lithe. She wears a form-fitting grey suit. Her hair grows low on her brow in a widow's peak. She has red irises.

'Don't be fooled by their youth!' The megaphone man must imagine he's in front of a full stadium, rather than a handful of saddos with gambling problems. 'These girls know how to rumble!'

A different guy has taken up the vacant position next to me. He whistles loudly with two fingers up to his mouth.

'All right!' he yells.

'What are they?' I ask him.

He looks at me with surprised and bleary eyes. 'Hellcats, man. You never seen a hellcat before?' He lifts his head and screeches to the sky, 'HOT LADIES!'

An air-siren goes off, and the two girls run at each other, colliding in midair. The guy next to me keeps whistling so piercingly I have to move. I kick through the dust, head down, pretending I can't feel adrenaline tingling along my limbs. Why would Paul come to a place like this? And why wouldn't he tell me about it?

'Wolfboy!' The call comes from the bleachers. I pick out a waving hand on the top step.

The bleachers are ancient and the wooden slats bend ominously underfoot as I make my way to the top.

'Wolfboy, my man!'

Tony wears a loud purple shirt and a gold necklace. He pulls me in to clap me on the back. 'I always wondered why I never see you here.'

'First time,' I say. Tony managed a cafe where Thom, Paul and I used to hang out, before the Darkness.

Tony whistles. 'You've been missing out. I'm having a good night.' He pulls a roll of cash from his shirt pocket. The chunky watch on his wrist flashes; so does the gold ring on his fingers. 'I'm up two grand and counting.'

'I didn't realise gambling was such a big thing in Shyness.'

Tony puts the cash away. 'Yeah, there's the money side, but really people just like to see people beat the shit out of each other.'

'People?' I say. 'Don't you mean freaks? People like watching the freaks beat the shit out of each other.'

Tony punches my shoulder affectionately. 'Don't be a hater.'

I ignore that. 'You ever seen Paul at these fights?'

'Your skinny Korean friend? Yeah, sometimes. One time he got me to place a bet for him. But I haven't seen him for a few months.'

The thought that Paul hasn't told me about this makes me feel sick. He's been hiding parts of his life for longer than I thought. Tony bends his head as a hulking man comes to whisper in his ear. He introduces us.

'Wolfboy, this is the Gentleman. The brains behind all of this.'

I shake the Gentleman's hand. Brains are not what first spring to mind. He's at least a foot taller than me, bare-chested and hairy, wearing pinstriped pants held up with braces. What are they feeding these guys? He has a thick moustache and his hair is slicked back.

'Pleased to meet you, Wolfboy,' the Gentleman says in a polite bass. His meaty hands envelop mine. A mobile phone rings and Tony fumbles in his pocket. The Gentleman cuffs him over the head.

'Tony, turn that thing down. You trying to deafen me?'

'Sorry, sorry.' Tony walks away from us, with his phone stuck to his ear.

I turn back to the Gentleman. His gaze is disturbingly direct. 'Wolfboy, I won't beat around the bush. I came over to see if you're interested in fighting for me. We could do with someone like you.'

'Fresh blood?'

When the Gentleman smiles the sharpness of his teeth is terrifying. 'You could say that. Hopefully there won't be too much blood involved.'

'I don't think so.' My eyes shoot off towards the lit-up cage where the hellcat bout is reaching fever pitch. I remember fighting Doctor Gregory's henchmen on the rooftop in Orphanville. The crunch of bones under my fingers, the voltage rush and then, soon after, the nausea and guilt. 'I'm not much of a fighter.'

'With all due respect, Wolfboy, I know a fighter when I see one.'

I don't want to argue with him. Something about his manner, or the way he holds himself, reminds me of Gram. He's probably the same age as Gram would be if he were alive. The Gentleman leans in closer. I smell liquor and dust and clothes that don't get washed often.

'You think you're carrying a burden. But it's a privilege.'

'What am I?' I dare to whisper.

'It's worse if you don't give in.' The Gentleman's mouth is at my ear. 'I heard from my little hellcat that the Doctor has been sniffing around you. Do not trust that man.'

'I don't.'

The Gentleman puts his hand on my shoulder. A kind touch, worlds apart from the cuff he gave Tony. 'The Doctor is nothing but a charlatan, Wolfboy. A megalo-maniac with ambitions to run this suburb. But he can only have the power you give him, nothing more. Whatever he's told you, it's all lies.'

'He hasn't told me anything. And if he did I wouldn't believe him.'

'Good.' The Gentleman straightens suddenly. Tony is heading our way. The Gentleman raises his voice again. 'Think about it. You can earn good money.'

The shouting and barracking over by the cage has become cacophonous.

'All right, Wolfboy?' asks Tony, clapping me on the back again. We look out over the top of the crowd. Something is happening near the cage. People are piling together. I see punches thrown, and bottles cracked over heads.

'Please excuse me,' says the Gentleman as he leaves. 'Wolfboy, come see me again. Soon.'

Tony surveys the growing brawl.

'Feral,' he says. It's difficult to know if he says it with censure or approval.

From my vantage point I can see the Gentleman heading into the thickest knot of spectators. He tosses people out of his way as if they don't weigh a thing. Once he reaches the centre, far from trying to stop the fighting, he starts kicking and headbutting anything in sight.

'I'm going,' I tell Tony.

'Sure, sure.' Tony doesn't take his eyes off the fighting.

Dust flies up in the floodlights. The two hellcats are pacing idly in the cage, watching what's happening outside. I have one more question before I leave. I would have asked the Gentleman if we hadn't been interrupted.

'What do you know about the Datura Institute, Tony?'

That surprises him. He turns to me.

'Don't bother with that shit, Wolfboy,' he says. 'Why would you bother with that? The Datura is the opposite of this.'

I straighten, letting Tony see my full height. 'You know everything that goes on in Shyness. Tell me how I can talk to some blue people.'

The night has been long, almost as long as that first night with Wildgirl, and I feel like the walking dead by the time I get home. There's a light on in Blake's room. The temptation to sag onto the couch is strong, but—

'Blake?' I knock even though I can already see her surrounded by her usual flotilla of books and pencils. A charcoal smudge crosses her left cheek. A large sheet of paper covered in black scratches lies on her bed. I sit down and turn the paper around.

'Ravens,' she says. 'Or raven. There's one that visits our backyard every few days. Sometimes he brings a friend.'

I turn the paper back the right way. 'So did Diana behave herself the other night?'

Blake turns her attention back to her book. 'Yes.'

'What did you do with her?'

'We made a cubby. Pizzas.' Blake twists a piece of hair round and round her finger, then lets it spiral.

'Did you play in the backyard?'

'No.'

'Did you go anywhere else?' She frowns at her quilt cover and doesn't answer. 'Blake?'

Blake finally looks at me. She looks scared. The scars on her arms, a legacy of her time with the Kidds, are visible below her lion t-shirt. 'Tell me what my punishment is,' she says.

That knocks the wind out of me. 'I'm not going to do that. You're not in the Kidds anymore. There's no... punishment.'

'I didn't think you would be angry.'

'I'm not angry,' I say automatically, but it's a lie. I get a brief and unpleasant memory-flash of what my father often looked like. Tight all over, a zigzag vein popping out on his temple. 'Why would you take Diana out of the house? Who's the Queen of the Night?'

'Diana wanted to meet her. I told her how cool she is.'

'Who is she? What's her real name?'

'I didn't know it was wrong.'

I sigh. 'Blake, Diana's a little girl. You can't give her everything she wants. And you'd have to know that

Ortolan wouldn't want you out in the dark. Where does the Queen live? Shyness?'

Blake nods. She looks chastened but at least the fear is gone.

'Why is she called that?'

Blake's eyes dart to the side. 'I don't know. Because of her job, maybe.'

'Her job,' I repeat, but Blake doesn't elaborate. 'Is this the friend you were going to show the tarsier to?'

She doesn't answer. I wait a few seconds. There's more I want to know, but I don't want to push Blake. She hasn't had a normal family life for a while, if ever. I don't know too much about what happened before the Kidds.

I pat the paper on her bed. 'I like the ravens.'

Her relief is palpable. 'Do you want to play Monopoly?'

We've got a Monopoly set that we've doctored, with the street names changed to Shyness names, and Lego blocks glued on to make Orphanville. Blake always takes the bike token, and I use the tarsier we made out of tin foil.

'It's the middle of the night, Blake. As in, the night-night. I've got to get some sleep. Tomorrow, though, okay?'

I close Blake's door and use my last reserves of energy to drag my feet to the front room. I flop onto the couch, caring little that I land on top of a book. I pull out the ribbon Ortie gave me, letting it run through my fingers.

15

I make sure I'm ready for Mum when she gets up. I'm dressed in my school uniform, my bag packed with what I need for Shopping Night, sitting on the edge of the couch waiting. I've had barely five hours' sleep. School is going to hurt today.

Mum walks into the lounge with a toothbrush poking from the corner of her mouth. She fumbles with the clasp on her bracelet.

'You're keen for your first day,' she says. 'Honey, can you do this for me?'

I shake my head, refusing to acknowledge her outstretched wrist. Mum dumps the bracelet on the kitchen counter and pulls the toothbrush from her mouth.

'What's wrong? You're giving me that look.'

'Sit down,' I say.

'Oh god.' Her face falls, and she zips over to the couch in record time, staring at me with wide eyes. 'Are you pregnant? Don't tell me you're pregnant.'

'I'm not pregnant, Mum. Give me some credit, please. I want to talk about you.'

'Me?'

'I'm going to ask you something and I want you to tell me the truth, even if you think it's going to make me mad. I need to know.' I pause. Mum has two spots of white toothpaste on either side of her mouth, and she hasn't painted her face yet. 'A couple of months ago, say six months ago, did you answer my phone and talk to someone?'

She looks confused for a few seconds, then recognition dawns. 'Oh. That.'

'Yes, that. Teen wolf from Shytown. This is the bit where you tell me what the hell you were doing answering my phone, for one. And then another thing you might want to tell me: what did you say to him?'

Mum draws back into the couch. 'The thing is, Nia, I was protecting you. After that night, when you never came home and I was so worried, I realised that I hadn't been doing my job as a parent properly. So when he called, I thought the right thing to do, the proper, responsible thing to do—'

'MUM,' I say. 'Cut the crap. It is of vital importance that you tell me what you said to him.'

Mum shrinks even more. 'I told him that he wasn't good enough for my daughter and that he should never call you again.'

I stare into space for a few seconds, pressing my lips together. It's worse than I thought. No wonder Wolfboy was so vague about what was said. I speak with tight control. 'I'm going to go to school now, Mum. And I won't be coming with you to Fish Creek on Wednesday. I don't want to talk to you at the moment.'

'Nia,' she says, pleading, practically hanging onto the hem of my school dress.

'Nuh.' I hold my hand up in her face. 'That's enough.'

The walk through the school gates is loud, the yard is loud, assembly is loud. Hundreds of screaming teenagers all trying to tell each other everything they did on summer holiday, in the shortest space of time possible. A wave of body heat and body odour and hormones. The only good thing is that now I'm not the new girl anymore. I notice straightaway that there's a different vibe in classes. Everyone quietens down and takes notes, even the kids who are normally climbing the walls. I try to concentrate, I really do. But my head isn't really in school; it's still in front of the train station, in the dark and the cold, arguing with Wolfboy.

At lunchtime I grab a salad roll from the tuckshop and eat it quickly in the quad with the group of girls I made friends with last year. We talk about which boys got hotter over the summer, and which teachers we have this year. Even though the sun bakes the crown of my head so fiercely I might actually catch on fire, I can't stop thinking about the night.

I give up trying and go to the library to use the computer. We don't have the internet at home, a fact that never ceases to amaze my classmates. The library is deserted. Even the hardcore nerds aren't inside on the first day.

I search for Datura Institute, but nothing comes up. No big surprise. If you were running a clandestine organisation, you'd hardly have your own website. Next, I look up datura. As I'd suspected from the flowers on the card, it's a plant.

At first the information is boring and heavy with scientific terms. I scroll down to the juicier bits about witches brews and love potions and hallucinogens. Holy crap. Confirmation that some seriously weird shit goes down in Shyness. If Paul's involved in a secret society, they're just as likely to be into kitten sacrifice as flower arranging. If the institute is a front for a druggie cult, though, why would you give it such an obvious name? Maybe whoever runs it doesn't care. Police aren't exactly an issue in Shyness.

According to the site, many people have died, either

accidentally or deliberately, after eating the datura plant. I jump off the computer and head for the stacks. I'm an old-fashioned girl in more than a few ways and I'd rather look up a book than stare at a screen all day.

I scan through the science Deweys and eventually find some illustrations of datura plants, which look like delicate upside-down tubas. Apparently there are lots of different types, even though they all look basically the same. Their names are chilling: devil's trumpet, mad apple, moonflower, nightshade.

Wolfboy's right to be concerned. I look at the line drawings of the beautiful but deadly plants. Paul was a nice guy. Jury's still out on Wolfboy. I'd like to pretend I didn't care about either.

'You're not dressed,' is the first thing Helen says to me.

She's wearing a long, glittering silver caftan and, inexplicably, has a black moustache drawn on her upper lip, the ends curling up towards her cheeks. Behind her, the shop floor has already been cleared and a makeshift catwalk laid down.

'I came straight from school.' I hold up my backpack. 'My ballgown's in here.'

'Good girl.' Helen waves a champagne flute at me. Her whole body sways with her. 'Because I need something to go right tonight.'

'What's wrong?' I ask, as Ruth sweeps past me and snatches the glass out of Helen's hand.

'The caterer forgot our order,' Ruth says. 'But they're still going to put something together, and drop it off a bit later. Helen's nephew was supposed to DJ but he's stuck at the beach with a broken-down car. I've put together an emergency playlist for the parade, and we'll have to play store records for the rest of it. On the plus side, Bob has already built the stage, and we've had loads of last-minute RSVPs. Oh, but Duncan has food poisoning. So no male model.'

'Which is why Helen has a moustache?' I guess.

Ruth points at me. 'Bingo.'

'So, Helen is taking Duncan's place in the fashion show?'

I don't want to be rude, but Duncan is at least six feet tall and as thin as a Masai, whereas Helen is a five-foot-nothing all-woman.

Helen clearly agrees with my assessment of the situation, because she slaps her own arse so hard it makes her wince. 'This is prime rump steak, ladies! How'm I going to fit it into those skinny little man clothes?'

Ruth gives me a beseeching look, and starts pulling reams of fabric out of the storeroom. 'Please, Nia, can you get dressed quickly and help me with this train wreck? I left you something to wear in the staffroom.'

I race off to the staffroom where I find a red velour jumpsuit hanging on the door. It's much nicer than the fluffy old formal dress I was going to wear. I put it on and brush my hair out, slapping on a quick bit of mascara and lippie. There's a knock on the door.

'Have you got it on?' calls out Ruth. She pokes her head around the door. 'Ooh, I knew that would suit you. Let me quickly do your hair. I brought my curling iron.'

I sit on the kitchen table while Ruth gets to work behind me. The curling iron is warm against my scalp.

'Hey, I almost forgot—how did your big date go?'

'Don't ask.'

'Oh, sweetie. That bad?'

'Yeah.' I'm unable to say much more than that. Ruth's hands are soft against the nape of my neck. My hair crackles. 'But, you know, I'm going to study hard this year,' I tell her. 'And then rule the world after that. I don't need boys.'

'I don't doubt it. And now, magic has officially been worked. Although it's not difficult with hair as beautiful as yours.'

I check myself in the mirror. Ruth does have magic fingers. She's somehow managed to twist my hair into a sleek forties hairdo, my hair rolling away from my face on either side. I turn my head and see some lazy curls tumbling down my back.

When we emerge from the staffroom Helen has recovered from her despair and managed to cover all the windows with heavy drapes, put some breathy sixties French pop on the stereo, and pour a tray of champagne. She calls out from her position near the counter-slash-bar. 'Nia, darling! You're needed over here!'

It must be after five because the front part of the shop is filling up fast. Lots of people have dressed up for the occasion, in dresses and suits and flashy seventies disco wear. I squeeze past a man in a safari suit to get behind the counter.

'You have a visitor, honey,' Helen says.

I look across the counter and I see Wolfboy.

He's red in the face, from sunlight or embarrassment, I don't know.

'Nia,' he says. 'You look, um, incredible.'

I don't think I'm exaggerating to say that in this moment I am completely unable to produce sounds from my mouth. I look mutely across at Helen instead. Maybe if I pretend he's not here, I can make him disappear.

'I've already introduced myself to the gorgeous Jethro.' Helen's eyes twinkle even more than her caftan. She has the same look on her face that she gets when we bring her surprise doughnuts from the bakery.

'What are you doing here?' My voice is snappy.

'Ortolan gave me her invite.' Wolfboy holds up the

printed curl of ribbon Helen used as invitations.

'It's a pity she couldn't make it tonight,' Helen says, 'but I'm glad she sent someone in her place. Nia needs some more people her own age here, instead of all these old farts. Champagne?'

Wolfboy shakes his head. I have my arms crossed, mostly to force away the image I have of him leaving the Darkness in his black night-time clothes and pale skin, and crossing into the sunlight and heat of the City. Crammed into a smelly train carriage, walking down the bright summer streets, all to come here. To see me.

'So, you think I'm going to forgive you because you made a minor effort to find out where I work?'

Next to me Helen fusses with trays of glasses, but I can tell she's still listening. Listening with all her body, as if she could suck sound up through her pores.

Wolfboy's eyes are piercing blue and brimming with apologies.

'I'm sorry,' he says, hands fidgety on the glass-topped counter.

I look down at those hands, the too-thick hair growing there, a reminder that Wolfboy is not your average guy. Maybe my mum was right to protect me from him.

'There's nothing I can say other than that. I wanted so badly for the other night to go well, and it didn't.'

I teeter on the edge, staring back at him. He doesn't

flinch. He's brushed his hair and put on a neat button-down shirt for the journey. I have the barest thread of an idea forming in my mind.

'Exactly how sorry are you?' I say.

16

I take my place to the side of the catwalk, behind a microphone.

'Welcome to the Emporium Shopping Night Fashion Parade,' I say, following the cards Helen has written out for me. There are whoops and whistles. The guests have clustered around the stage, glasses in hand. 'Tonight we hope to show you that, like good wine, fashion only improves with age.'

I nod at Difficult Steve, his face lit blue from the laptop in front of him. It turns out he's our saviour, offering to take care of the music. A Serge Gainsbourg song filters out of the PAs.

'First up we have Ruth in a 1940s shirtwaist dress made

from silk shantung, with a matching bolero.'

On cue, Ruth slides out from behind a curtain and makes her way down the catwalk. The guests start clapping immediately, and Ruth smiles demurely at them, walking daintily in her dainty outfit.

'Ruth wears shoes taken from our large selection of vintage ladies' court shoes and carries a contemporary handbag made from recycled fabric.'

Ruth sashays right off the catwalk. I look down at the next card, which is full of corrections. I hope I can decipher it.

'Please welcome to the stage our male ubermodel Jethro, in a velvet riding jacket, pin-tucked silk shirt and tuxedo pants.'

Wolfboy creeps out from behind the curtain and stands at the head of the runway. Ruth has coaxed his hair into a short ponytail. The tuxedo pants are waaaaay snug against his legs, and the maroon jacket hugs his torso. The silk shirt froths at his throat. He should be riding a stallion across the moors.

I forget for a moment that there's a microphone right in front of my mouth.

'Wow,' I say, and there are laughs and whistles. Wolfboy scowls at me, ruining his dashing look. I nod at him and he traipses down the runway. At first he's stiff and awkward, but the audience is so enthusiastic that by the time he reaches the end he actually seems to be enjoying himself. He pulls a department store catalogue pose, hands on hips, squinting off into the distance, and then starts the return journey. He catches my eye with a grin and a wink, and I know he's forgiven me for putting him up for public spectacle. I clutch my chest and place my hand melodramatically against my forehead—*be still, my beating heart!* Only I'm not acting, not acting at all.

The smell of mothballs and perfume is strong behind the fur coat rack. But I don't care because Wolfboy is next to me, warm by my side. We've dragged a couple of cushions behind the rack, and the only thing giving our hiding place away is Wolfboy's long legs poking out the bottom. Downstairs the cash register dings regularly. I'd feel guilty for slacking off, only it was Helen who sent us upstairs with a bottle of champagne, mumbling something about them not making boys like that when she was young.

Wolfboy hands me the bottle with a grimace. 'Too sweet.'

'I know I am,' I say, and put the bottle aside. I don't need to be fuzzy tonight. The mezzanine floor hums with bass underneath us. 'Look, I also owe you an apology. I asked my mum about your phone call.'

'It's okay.'

'No, it's not really. There's all the privacy stuff to begin with, but mostly she shouldn't have said those things to you. And I want you to know that I would have called you back if I'd known.'

'It's done now. Let's forget about it. I'm glad'—Wolfboy ducks his head—'I'm glad we're sitting here now. Even if it does smell like a grandma convention.'

In the low light I catch the silvery shine of something against Wolfboy's shirt.

'Is that what I think it is?' I reach out and snag it. It's Wolfboy's lighter, and it used to belong to his brother Gram. It's engraved with Gram's and Ortolan's initials. I flip it over in my hand. 'So this is what we almost died for.'

'We didn't almost die.' Wolfboy leans forward so the chain doesn't pull on his neck.

'It felt like it.' I let go of the lighter.

I remember our escape from Orphanville in the dusty tunnels and crying when I saw Wolfboy again. I'd left him on the roof with Doctor Gregory and his two body-guards. When he finally made it down to the tunnel I was so relieved. Everything felt so much *more* that night, as if we were starring in one hell of a realistic movie.

'What happened up there with Doctor Gregory?' I ask.

'I told you, didn't I?'

'Not really. You told me you jumped up on the wall and ran around the edge of the roof, and that you fought his bodyguards.'

'That's all true.' Wolfboy takes the champagne, but then doesn't drink, peeling off a corner of the label instead. 'But I didn't tell you what Doctor Gregory said to me. He said that he knew why I was different. And then he mentioned an institute.'

An unpleasant stillness settles over me. I remember now, Wolfboy telling me he thought we'd been lured to Orphanville deliberately, that Doctor Gregory didn't care about the lighter at all. I add that to what I learned last night about Paul and the Datura Institute.

'Do you think he's using Paul to get to you?'

Wolfboy shrugs. 'For all I know, it was Paul who went to him in the first place. I haven't heard from Doctor Gregory in all this time.'

'What. Did. He. Want. With. You?' I get so worked up I slap his thigh for punctuation. Wolfboy turns his head and looks at me, blue eyes to brown. 'I don't know how things go in Shyness, but out there in the real world, grown men don't show this much interest in nineteen-year-olds who aren't their sons.'

'I've got no idea.'

Wolfboy produces a book from his pocket. I part the coats to let in more light so I can read, '*SHYNESS: A young lady's treatise.*'

'Look at the author's name.'

'Gregory,' I breathe. 'Related?'

'No idea. It's a common name. But look at this.'

The page he shows me has a photograph of a young girl posed in an old-fashioned white dress. Her hand rests stiffly on a chair; ribbons gather at the side of her head. It's difficult to tell her age because of the layer of wispy dark hair covering her entire face. It thins only around her eyes and mouth. She's bucktoothed to an unfortunate degree.

The caption reads: *Infamous wild-child Nora Gregory.*

Wolfboy reads out the facing text. He has a halting, uncertain way of reading that makes me want to climb into his lap and stroke his cheek. '*"Despite being afflicted with Night Sickness in her youth my grandmother, Nora, went on to marry and produce five children. Whilst there were a handful of similar Night Sickness cases during the Third Night, my grandmother's affliction was by far the most severe on record."*'

'Huh,' I say. 'Well, she is way hairier than you.' I take the book out of his hands.

The girl stares into the camera, almost with defiance.

'She doesn't look sick, and you don't seem sick either. Is there anything else about her?'

'That's it. It jumps straight to planetary orbits after that. It's a strange book. This girl Delilah's diary and a history of Shyness at the same time. I found it a few days ago.'

I thumb through the book until I find a section of journal entries. I read in a posh English accent. For some reason I always assume people long ago all spoke with posh English accents. '"*Sometimes I feel like little Kay in the Snow Queen, who swallowed a shard of the devil's mirror, and could only see ugliness in the world. Only I have swallowed a portion of shadow, and that is why I feel the way I do."*'

Wolfboy doesn't smile as I expect him to. He takes the book back. There's a pause.

'I was never going to actually go into the Datura Institute,' I say. 'I was trying to get a reaction out of you.'

'Well, it worked.'

I find Wolfboy's hand in the darkness and grip his fingers. 'What do you want to do now?'

'I haven't seen Paul since Saturday night. Finding him seems more important than figuring out this other stuff.' The heaviness shows in Wolfboy's voice.

'I agree.'

'After I saw you last night I ran into this guy I know, Tony. He told me that the blue people go to this club Umbra on Wednesdays.'

'I hope Paul turns up before then. But if he doesn't, that can be our next step.'

I hesitate, remembering my words earlier to Ruth about studying hard and not needing boys. Did I really believe that, even when I was saying it? I take a deep breath and tell him anyway. 'My mum is going away on Wednesday for a few days, and I'm home alone. I can come over to

Shyness without having to make excuses. Our neighbour will be watching me, but I can stretch the rules a little.'

I kick open the coats again. There's no air in here.

Wolfboy turns to me. I have a curiously mixed-up picture of him in my head, half memory of the velvet-jacketed, ponytail dandy, and half what's in front of me now, Shyness boy in black jeans.

'Why do you want to help me?'

'I'm an investigative journalist writing a secret article about Shyness,' I say. 'And you're my main source.'

I'm hoping he'll move closer, but instead he holds up his blue-lit phone. 'It's Blake,' he says. 'Paul's come home.'

17

I'm still arguing my case, even as Wolfboy unlocks his door. I'm so busy talking I barely register how odd it is to be at his house again.

'Why can't you talk to Paul yourself?'

'I'm no good at talking, you know that.'

The house is as quiet as it was the first time I was here. There's a light on in the front room.

Wolfboy lowers his voice. 'Paul likes you. I'll say the wrong thing.'

'Paul hardly knows me,' I say, as I follow him into the lounge room. A girl is curled up on the couch, book in hand. She's moon-pale even by Shyness standards. At first I think I don't know her, but then I realise I do.

'Blake, do you remember Nia?'

I wave. 'Hi, Blake.'

'Wildgirl, hi.' She looks at me through an owlish pair of specs. 'You came back.'

'I couldn't keep away.' Blake has changed from the scared girl I met those months ago. Now she's dressed in clothes that fit her and she talks directly to me. Her skin and eyes are clear.

'You look so pretty,' she says.

I look down at my jumpsuit. I'd forgotten I was all dolled up still from the Shopping Night. 'Thanks. It's a killer going to the toilet in this thing, though.'

'Where is he?' asks Wolfboy.

Blake folds her book and sits up. 'In his room. I tried to talk to him when he came in, but…I moved in here so that I'd know if he left the house again. What are you going to do?'

'Nia's going to talk to him.'

'No, I'm not.'

'What was the point of you coming with me then?'

He's right. I should be making my way home already instead of trailing him.

'He won't talk to me about his ex, but he might to you.'

'Her name was Ingrid,' says Blake.

'And then try and casually slip something in about the Datura Institute and Doctor Gregory,' Wolfboy adds.

'Oh, that's going to sound real natural.'

'They *did it*,' says Blake. 'Paul had never done it with anyone before.'

Oh, good god. Way too much information. I throw my hands up. 'All right, everyone chill. I'm going in.'

I walk up the dark hallway. Paul's door is ajar. Words cannot describe how awkward and stupid I feel tapping on it. When he doesn't answer I push it gently open. He's sitting on his bed in darkness, looking at his phone, music playing quietly in the background. At first glance he doesn't look capable of causing everyone so much worry.

'Hey,' I say, which I figure is an okay place to start.

Paul looks up. He locks his phone and tosses it on the bed. It's too dark to see his face properly.

'Remember me? Wildgirl? We danced up a storm at Little Death that one time?'

After a pause, Paul answers. 'What are you doing here?' His words are slow and thick, but the question is smart. I'm counting on him not being smart enough to figure out that this whole scenario is a little weird. It's so obvious I'm Wolfboy's messenger.

'Just visiting,' I say, keeping it simple.

Tiny speakers sit to the side of the bed, producing tinny music. The chorus to this song sounds like it goes: pain, pain, pain, pain, pain. Paul doesn't look at me sitting cross-legged next to his mattress.

'Where's Jethro?' he asks. As if on cue Wolfboy walks across the floor overhead. An electric guitar starts up. We planned it that way so Paul would know Wolfboy wasn't eavesdropping on us.

'Not sure,' I say, shrugging. 'Around. Do you mind if I switch on a lamp?' I don't wait for permission.

The light gives me a chance to see what everyone has been fussing about. Paul's black hair could have been cut with gardening shears and he's scarecrow skinny. But the real clincher is when he finally turns to me. His beautiful amber eyes look like cloudy honey. He's seeing me without really seeing me. His sockets are lined with deep purple, the only spot of colour on his moon-tanned skin.

'Lady In Red.' He stares at my velvet jumpsuit. 'Am I awake?'

'I don't know, you tell me: are you?'

'There's a girl in my bedroom, so it must be a dream.'

'What about the other girl?' I ask, crossing my fingers in case I'm being too blunt.

Paul frowns, struggling to remember, or understand what I've asked him. Behind his struggle is the backdrop of music. The chorus is definitely the word 'pain' yelled over and over again, and the verses are pure wailing.

'Ingrid?' I say, when it becomes clear Paul can't or won't remember.

Paul flushes with delight when I say her name, but a

split second later his expression is of pure despair. A tear rolls down his pale cheek.

'I don't understand,' he says.

'Don't understand what?'

'I don't understand,' he repeats. He beats the heel of his hand against his forehead. 'It doesn't make sense. First she says it's there, and then she says it's not there. Where did it go?'

I pull Paul's hand away from his face. 'Everyone is so worried about you, Paul. They're worried you're caught up in something bad.'

'I've done bad things.' Paul looks me in the eye, and for a moment his gaze is certain and true. 'He'll never forgive me.'

'Who won't forgive you?'

But Paul has flown off again. Into space, into orbit, looking at the ceiling.

'I want to forget,' he says.

I sigh. This is almost impossible. Paul brushes his hands over his sleeping bag, making it whisper. I can't think of another way to get through to him so I start talking, hoping that somehow a few of my words will sink in.

'Paul, you're obviously going through a tough time. But you have friends who care about you. So, whatever you've been doing recently, it doesn't matter. You could tell them. Or me, if you want. If you talked about how you were feeling it might make you feel better. You shouldn't be spending time with people who don't know you. Like these blue people, how do you know they...'

I trail off. Paul has stopped smoothing the sleeping bag. Have I said too much?

'Do you want to see a photo of her?' He fumbles to find his phone in the folds of his bed.

'Sure,' I say, surprised.

Paul presses something on his phone and then hands it to me. He's having another moment of clarity. 'I deleted them all. But I had to keep one. Just one.' Paul shuts his eyes as if he's praying. 'No one tells you how much it hurts. The insides of my body are bleeding. I'm being ripped apart. I can feel it. It's not in my head. My whole body hurts.'

Ingrid and Paul are sitting together at a party in someone's backyard. They look like they're anything but hurting. Paul smiles at the camera, his arm draped over her shoulders. Ingrid looks off to the side, laughing at something or someone out of view. She's elfin and pretty, with short dark hair and a sparkle about her.

'She's gorgeous.' I touch the screen to zoom in on her. A weird menu flashes up over the top of the photo. Paul's phone is heaps fancier than mine. I tap the menu irritably. Go away, bossy menu. The screen goes black and then a photo comes up again. But it's not the same one.

I get a sick feeling in the very bottom of my stomach.

I press arrows back and forth, trying to find the photo of Paul and Ingrid. But it's gone. There are other photos clearly taken at the same party, of other people, but not that one. I've deleted it.

The sick feeling grows. 'Um, Paul, I think there's a problem with your phone?'

He snatches it from my hands and scrolls frantically. 'What have you done?'

'I'm sorry,' I say. 'Your phone is so confusing, I think I might have accidentally—'

Paul throws himself at me, knocking me flat on the carpeted floor. I attempt to sit up, but Paul is above me, trying to pin my arms by the side of my head. I can't believe he has any strength at all in his twiggy arms.

'Cow.' His eyes are wild, his face an avalanche.

I get scared. Not for myself, but for him. He lets go of my arms to slap my face, and I use the opportunity to pull his hair. He yelps and gets hold of my fingers, bends them backwards. I scream.

I half-sit up and kick my legs, hoping that I'll manage to kick him in the nads, but we've reached a stalemate: I can't throw him off, and he won't let me up. I'm out of breath. I'm the worst fighter in the world and Paul is not much better.

I give up and fall backwards, not caring anymore if

Paul wants to hit me. Somewhere during this the electric guitar upstairs has stopped. Paul notices it too, because he pushes away from me and runs from the room.

I look backwards, arching my neck to see an upside-down Blake in the doorway, flapping her arms and saying 'Oh, oh, oh' like a demented bird, over and over again. There's the sound of boots in the hallway, then Wolfboy replaces her.

A rush of cold air from the open front door sweeps up the hallway.

'I'll kill him,' he says. But instead of chasing Paul out the door, he sinks to his knees and helps me up.

eighteen

Diana sits in her bedroom nook, basking in the sunlight pouring through the bay window. Heart-shaped sunglasses cover half her face, and her crayons spill over her lap. A sheet cut from Ortolan's giant roll of paper carpets the floor.

'I can't draw when you're looking,' she complains. The corners of her mouth are green where she's nibbled on a crayon. 'You're not supposed to look until it's finished.'

'Okay, okay.' I move the folding Chinese screen so she's hidden from sight. After the drama with Blake the other night Ortolan wanted us to stay in today. I thought it was a sensible idea, but I'm already restless. All Diana wants to do is draw.

'I'm going to sit over here in Mummy's chair and read.'

'You don't read,' Diana says, with absolute certainty from behind the screen.

'I do now.'

Before I can open Delilah's book, my phone vibrates in my pocket.

'Back in a minute, Flopsy,' I tell Diana, then start down the stairs.

'Hello?' A smile is already spreading across my face. I stop halfway down the stairs.

'Wolfie.'

'How are you? Are you feeling okay? Did you sleep all right?'

'Yeah, I'm fine. Stop worrying about me. Everyone at school thinks I got in a scrag fight, and now no one will mess with me for the rest of the year. That's a good thing.'

I want to apologise a hundred times over for yesterday, but I kill the words. Nia told me last night that I needed to stop saying sorry before I became really annoying.

I can't help wondering where Paul is, even though I want to pretend I don't care. I've pictured all the places he might be. The cottage? The creek? Little Death? Maybe I should have chased after him, but I didn't want to leave Nia after I'd basically fed her to the lions.

'You're at school now?' I ask.

Even though I hated school before I dropped out, I

have a momentary flash of envy. There's something simple about showing up on time and doing what you're told. I wouldn't mind someone bossing me through the average day in Shyness, telling me what to do.

'Yeah.' I hope I'm not imagining that her voice holds a smile to match mine. 'I snuck out of sixth period Maths. I'm in the loo.'

'Classy.'

She laughs. 'Listen, I'm going to go to work after school tomorrow night and pick up what we need. Then I'll go home, hopefully having cleverly avoided my mum, then come to you.'

There's nothing I want more than to spend more time with her, but not like this.

'Wolfie? You've gone quiet. Are you having second thoughts?' Wildgirl asks. Her voice is hesitant. 'Because I want you to know, I'm not.'

I think she means Paul, and not me and her. I don't have second thoughts about her, other than mild terror at setting myself up for a huge fall when she decides she's not interested after all.

'I'm causing trouble between you and your mum again.'

She snorts. 'You're not causing the trouble. She is.'

'But…should we even help Paul?' I sit down on the stairs. 'How long have you known him?'

'Since…forever. Since kindergarten.'

For as long as I can remember, Paul has been there. All through primary school and high school and Gram dying and my parents leaving, he's been there. If you'd asked me a few days ago I would have said that he was the least likely person I know to hit a girl. And while I'm still mad at him, I'm also mad at myself for not realising he was hurting so bad from breaking up with Ingrid.

'He's your oldest friend. And from the sounds of it this is the first time he's been a real idiot. So if you do the sums, that's fifteen years of being an awesome friend, minus a few weeks of being a knob.'

'You're right.' I think I can hear the sound of doors banging shut and hand dryers blasting.

Her voice drops to a whisper. 'Hey, listen, I think class just ended. Call me later and we'll work out the exact details.'

Diana hasn't kicked up a fuss yet, so I stay sitting on the stairs and pull out Delilah's book. I thumb through it, looking for something that might hint that she's related to Doctor Gregory. Looking for anything, really.

I find a section peppered with sepia photographs of Shyness. A photo of a bluestone building topped with soaring spires is captioned: *St Paul's Cathedral, Shyness.*

'That's strange.' There's no cathedral in Shyness. We had a chapel at my high school, but it was built in the seventies. There might be one or two brick churches, now filled with squatters, but there's no cathedral.

This is the last known photograph of the cathedral in Daylight. In the last period of Eternal Night (1857–1864), more than twenty people jumped from the main spire of St Paul's. In December of 1863 the spire was demolished and the cathedral decommissioned. The decision was criticised after Daylight returned in March the following year, ending what had been the Third Night.

I examine the edges of the photo for evidence of the cathedral's location, but there's nothing to give it away. *The last period of Eternal Night. Third Night.*

I look up blankly. I paid too much attention to the photo of the furry girl the other day, and not enough attention to the words.

There's been Darkness in Shyness before.

I'm glad I'm already sitting down, because I feel as if the world just shifted on its axis.

If what Delilah wrote is true, there's been three other periods of Darkness. I never paid much attention when I was at school, but I'm certain we never covered this particular part of Shyness history. Why don't people talk about it?

I hear Diana's footsteps overhead.

I look back at the page. The image of people jumping from a cathedral spire is awful.

Could Delilah have been crazy, or making this up?

She does have the last name Gregory, after all. Maybe the whole clan are chronic liars.

'Jet-ro,' Diana calls from the top of the stairs.

She's finished her picture and laid it out on the floor of the main room. The paper is at least a metre wide and covered in coloured scribbles and shapes. Diana's drawings normally huddle in the corners, as if obeying a tilting gravity, but this one covers the paper evenly. I help her pin the edges down with tins of paint and the sticky tape dispenser. Diana regards her masterpiece with a pleased sigh. It takes some effort to push aside what I've just read and focus on her drawing.

'You want to tell me about it, Flopsy?'

I squat to have a closer look. A woolly purple cloud takes up almost the whole top half of the paper. A girl with wings flies below it, a big semi-circle smile taking up half of her head. Beneath that there's a patch of spiky trees. On the right there's a house with three people standing next to it. And a teapot, a cat, and a giant flower coming out of the ground.

I point to the flying girl. She likes me to guess what's what. 'Is that you?'

Diana nods.

I point to the purple cloud next. It's large, but there's still a lot of white paper left around it. 'Is that the Darkness?'

'No.' Diana squats too, folding her stumpy legs up with far greater ease than me. 'That's a dream. I flew out of the dream.' She puts a hand down on the cloud and turns to look at me with her big blues. Her fingers are psychedelic with crayon wax. 'I didn't get born, I ran out of a dream. They tried to chase me back, but I hid from them.'

I screw my face up in the exaggerated way that makes her laugh. 'That's crazy, Di-Di.'

She sets her mouth stubbornly. 'It's what happened. I remember it.'

'Who's this?' I ask, pointing to a pair of disembodied eyes hiding among the clump of trees.

'It's the Queen.'

'Oh yeah, the Queen of the Night?' I keep my voice casual. I haven't tried to ask about the other night. I was saving that line of questioning for later, when I'm stuffing her full of pancakes. Diana claps a hand over her mouth, her eyes wide above it.

'Blake told you not to tell anyone, right?'

She keeps her hand in place.

'What does the Queen of the Night do? Why is she hiding?' I try again, but there's no point. Diana has clammed up. I move on to the three people next to the house.

'That's Mummy, and me, and you?' I guess.

'That's me. I am here two times. And Mummy.' She

points to the person I thought was me dressed all in black. It's true he doesn't look anything like me, but sometimes that's no barrier in Diana's drawings. 'And the man.'

'What's wrong with his face?' I squint. The man has a pink scribble over his head.

'Splotchy,' says Diana.

I remember the man standing outside a few days ago, looking up at the window, and the red birthmark near his eye. The darkitect.

'This is the man we saw the other day out front, isn't it, Diana? Did you see him again? Have you ever talked to him?'

'Don't talk so fast, Jethro!' Diana bites her finger. 'You're confusing me!'

'I'm just curious,' I say, slower and quieter. 'Why is that man in the picture?'

Diana stands up and looks at me, mulish and resentful. 'I want pancakes,' she says. 'I want them NOW.'

On the way home, thinking about Diana's scribbly darkitect, and the night coming and going like the seasons, I find something strange huddled on the doorstep of a shop. A collection of teacups, with plants growing inside.

The plants are translucent, a colourless white. Stems like zombie fingers emerging from the dirt. Their bowed heads are laden with paper-thin petals. It's dark all round, but the tiny plants emit a determined glow. They're completely different to the ones I saw near the Green Lantern Lounge, but it has to be the same person, or group of people, leaving them.

I pick up two cups, one for Nia, one for Diana, and continue home.

nineteen

The alleyway is barely wide enough for one person. The buildings on either side rise high into the air. A bare ribbon of sky is visible overhead. The brick expanse to my right is graffitied from gravel to sky. I look for my favourite piece: six-foot-high white letters spelling out the word AMOEBA. Paul did it during his brief rebellious phase, around the time we all dropped out of school. But when I get to that section of wall, all that's visible under newer graffiti is EBA. Someone has defaced my favourite defacement.

Paul, Thom and I always used to sneak in the back way to Umbra, to avoid the long queues, and because we were too cheap to pay the cover charge.

Nia follows me with her hand on my shoulder, and Blake brings up the rear. We walk in silence. The service entrance finally appears. I usher Nia and Blake across an empty concrete cavern. Even in here, the floor vibrates with bass.

I stop in front of a truck-sized doorway curtained with thick strips of opaque plastic. There's light on the other side, leaking through. The thump-thump-thump of the music gets stronger. I turn to Nia and Blake, ready to deliver a serious speech about our aims for the evening, only to find them both standing there with equally inane grins on their faces.

'I forgot how stupid you look,' Blake says.

I look at my pale blue shirt and navy pants, then at Nia and Blake. They're dressed similarly to me, in outfits borrowed from Nia's work. Blake's clothes are too big and mine are too small. Nia's are just right.

'Speak for yourself,' I say to Blake.

Nia smiles and taps the bridge of her nose, until I remember I'm wearing Blake's nerd glasses and a baseball cap. Oh, right. I *do* look stupider than them.

'Lighten up.' She pinches my cheeks. 'Look at you. Your face is all frowny.'

'I don't want to be recognised.'

'We're just having a night out. So what if we're dressed strange? We find out what we can. It's acting. We can do that.'

I nod, trying to let her convince me. I'm pleased she's here, but I'm too wound-up to show it. She seems to be suffering no ill effects from Paul's attack, and she's not pissed off at him, or me. And she's ready to throw herself into the fray as an imposter blue person.

'Will you call me Wildgirl?' she asks. 'It's my stage name.'

'Sure. Can we discuss some rules, though?' I fold my arms and address them both. 'Do not leave the club for any reason. Do not tell anyone your real name. And we meet in an hour outside the toilets. Have your phones on vibrate and call in an emergency.'

'Yes, Dad,' says Nia. She knows she looks cute in her blue pyjamas, and she's taking advantage of it. She puts her hand forward. 'Come on, let's do a yay team!'

Blake immediately puts her hand on top of Nia's.

'I'm not doing that,' I say.

'Wolfie, do not deny us this simple pleasure. C'mon.'

I roll my eyes and put my hand on top of theirs.

'Yay team!' squeals Blake. And she's supposed to be the sensible one.

Umbra is a tsunami of intense surgical light and ear-splitting beats. The bass frequency thumps in my chest, tightening my throat. The room is a mess of sweaty dancing people. I didn't expect it to be this crowded.

I thought that Umbra wasn't as popular as it used to be. I was completely wrong.

'Why the hell is it so light in here?' Nia clutches my arm.

'It's always like this!' I shout. Behind Nia, Blake is frozen like a very small scientist in car headlights. She clutches her notebook to her chest.

'You right?' I ask her. 'Remember the Kidds have gone.'

Blake puts on a brave face. I use my finger to indicate we should do laps. Between Nia and Blake we might not even last the hour in here. I grab Nia's hand and drag her through the crowd.

Umbra is painted stark white all over, floors, walls, ceiling. There are lethal metal hooks running on tracks that cover the length of the ceiling, left over from the meatworks, and heavy chains hanging down from above. Dancers wearing little more than leather swimwear climb the chains. The sound system is so extreme it feels as if I'm going to be pushed over by its sheer volume.

Nia gets used to the light and sound remarkably swiftly, because by the time we find a step to sit on, she's moving her feet and starting to sway a little.

'Nuh-uh,' I say. I've seen her dance before, at Little Death. She knows how to move, and I like watching her move, but— 'We're not here to dance, we're here to find blue people.' I catch a glimpse of Blake looking up at the chain dancers in their skimpy outfits, her mouth open. I point it out to Nia.

'You think she'll be okay?' she asks.

'Sure. She's tougher than she looks. She had to be to survive the Kidds.' I have to sit really close to Nia to make myself heard. I sneak a look at her while she watches Blake. She's counteracted the drabness of the blue uniform with glittery blue eye shadow and two small silver sequins stuck next to each eye. I don't know if it's the bass making my heart pound or something else.

When I spoke to her last night I lay with the phone down next to me on the pillow. It sounded as if she was lying right beside me when I closed my eyes. It was a nice illusion.

'You know, after that night,' she'd said, her voice wispy over the phone line. 'It felt as if everything in my life was rebooted. So I asked my mum again about my dad. I didn't get angry this time. I asked nicely. And she told me about him.'

'What did she tell you?'

'She said she got together with him when she was really young. She was working as a waitress and he was the chef. When she got pregnant with me they tried to make it work, but it didn't take her long to realise he was a total arsehole. He used to hit her.'

'That's fucked,' I said.

'I know, right? So she wasn't hiding who he was to hurt me, she was doing it to protect me. Now that I know that, I can't believe I thought otherwise.'

'And she also wanted to forget about him,' I added, thinking also of Ortie and what she's told me about Gram, and how she went overseas to get away from the mess. The difference is, Gram would have never hit Ortie.

Going over this phone call now in my head, I realise something. I turn to Nia. 'Did you speak to your mum before she left?'

'No. I don't feel like forgiving her yet.'

'Well, don't leave it too long. You know what you told me last night, about your dad. It makes sense that your mum is overprotective.'

Nia makes a maybe-face, which morphs into something more alert. She leans in. 'Don't. Turn. Your. Head,' she says. 'We have blue people in the house.'

'Where?'

'Over there, on the dancefloor.'

I straighten up, and casually look to the right, adjusting my glasses so I can see properly. A cluster of blue-clad people dances among all the others. Looking at the real blue people I realise we look pretty authentic. I forgot for a minute what we're here to do.

'What do we do?' Nia sits up straight. 'Do we go talk to them?'

'Nope. We sit here and watch and play it cool.'

'What? No way. Let's go talk.'

She stands, and I drag her down.

'Trust me. It's better if we can get them to approach us. It'll seem more natural.'

'How are we gonna do that?' she asks.

'It's like when I first saw you at the Diabetic. I went up to you, but really you made the first move.'

'Shut up!' She remains unconvinced. 'How?'

I don't answer. I sit still. Then I look at her slyly out of the corner of my eye, before looking away. I look at her again, for longer this time, then drop my eyes. For my final look I stare, and bat my eyelashes provocatively.

I must do a good job because Nia laughs. It feels good to know I can do that.

'You look like such a dufus in those glasses! It's not sexy at all!' She puts her hands to her reddening face. 'Oh. Did I really do that?'

'It worked, didn't it?'

We look at each other too long, both smiling. I slide over, and then I put my hand up to her hair, lean in and place my mouth on hers. She parts her lips like she was expecting this, and we kiss. The glasses are crushing into my nose, so I pull them off quickly, not wanting to miss a second. I press myself closer until I can feel Nia's heat against me. Everything about her is so soft. I close my eyes and I'm nowhere at all. Drifting without gravity.

I have no idea how long we kiss for.

When I finally pull away, out of breath, Nia is still smiling at me.

'Hello, Wildgirl,' I say.

She sighs with satisfaction and leans against me, linking her pinkie finger with mine. We watch the dancefloor together. The cluster of blue people has drifted closer, moving almost directly in front of us.

Even though the music has got deeper and dirtier and faster, the blue people dance with their arms at their sides, looking at the floor. Most hop from side to side, completely out of time with the beat.

'They dance like Dreamers, don't you think?' Nia says. 'I know the music's different, but they move the same.'

One of the blue people hops until she faces us, lifts her head quickly and winks. It's Blake. I didn't recognise her at all. I'm suitably impressed. She's done much better than we have.

'Did you see that?' I ask. Nia nods.

'If Blake's on the job, do you think that means we can, you know?' She gives me a cheeky look with her blue-rimmed eyes. I lift her hand and kiss it.

'I think we shouldn't get too distracted.' I hate myself for saying it. 'We should pull our weight. Blake can't do everything.'

'Tonight's not all about us, is it?' she says close to my ear.

'You're still having a good time, though, aren't you?'

'Yeah, of course.' She turns to me. 'It's just different. That was then, this is now.'

20

I knock four times on the end cubicle, using the code: rat-TATAT-tat. The bathroom lights give my sore eyeballs a break. The music is so loud out there I'm pretty sure my insides are bleeding. Even in here the red walls vibrate.

'Blake!' Wolfboy stage-whispers when the door doesn't open. He's jumpy as hell, being in the ladies loos. He checks there's no one behind us. 'It's us. Come on.'

The door swings open. Blake still holds her notebook, a regular girl spy. She's not alone. There's a boy in blue clothes sitting on the closed toilet lid, blinking at us.

'Blake, you saucy minx,' I say. 'Should we leave you two alone?'

Blake flaps her notebook. 'Shhh. Come in.'

Wolfboy and I squeeze into the cubicle and lock the door. Quite frankly, I'm dismayed to find it necessary to stand very, very close to him. There's so little room in here that Blake has to sit on top of the cistern.

'Who is this?' Wolfboy asks.

'This is Sanjay.' Blake nudges the guy with her foot. 'Sanjay, these are my friends, uh, John and…Mary.'

She looks pleased at having thought up such convincing aliases.

'What's he doing in here?' Wolfboy is stressed out. He makes to pace up and down, before realising that he's got nowhere to go.

'Sanjay's from the institute. You know, like we are. Members.' She leans down and tugs on the sleepy Sanjay's arm. 'He loves it so much he even got this tattoo.' She shows us the inside of his wrist.

The two white flowers show up as ghosts on Sanjay's dark skin. They're datura flowers, identical to the flowers on the calling card Wolfboy showed me. Sanjay mumbles and yanks his hand away.

'I'm running late and I didn't study,' he says. 'I never learn. Should prepare.'

Blake turns to us, her plaits falling apart after the dancefloor. 'Who wouldn't love the Datura Institute, right? I mean, we all love to dream, right? That's why we go there to take part in the Program. To help with the *important sleep research*. And for the *good drugs*.'

Blake raises her eyebrows significantly. Luckily Sanjay is oblivious to her bad acting. I look impressed, pretty much because I am. Blake has come through with the goods.

I turn to Wolfboy and say quietly, 'Didn't I say they danced the same as Dreamers?'

His beautiful face is one big scowl. 'Paul hates Dreamers. Or at least he used to.'

'So, Sanjay is at a much higher level than us,' Blake interrupts. 'On the inside and stuff. He was telling me all sorts of interesting things about what they do with his dreams.'

'Pay in dreams.' Sanjay stares at the cubicle wall directly to his left. 'Harvest dreams, pay in dreams.'

'What does he mean?' Wolfboy asks Blake.

'I don't know. I can't figure it out. But he keeps saying that they take his dreams away.'

'Do you tell them about your dreams?' Wolfboy asks. 'Does Doctor Gregory write them down?'

That makes Sanjay titter. 'Collect. Record. Harvest like fruit. Put them in a jar.'

'What for?'

'Don't know. Don't care. I have them on loan and then I give them away.'

Wolfboy looks up at Blake. 'This is useless. He's too out of it.'

I look closely at Sanjay, who looks pretty young to be getting tattoos and messing with dreams. His mouth smiles but his eyes look worried. Wolfboy is right. Sanjay is totally out of it. I shuffle my feet. The floor is sticky and gross.

'I'm late for the exam.' Sanjay tries to stand up. 'I have to get top marks.'

'Wait, you haven't told them the most interesting bit.' Blake pushes him down. 'Sanjay, tell them about Paul.'

Sanjay rakes his cheek with his fingernails. 'Paul Kim. Teacher's pet. Paul Kim does not have to pay in dreams. Teacher's pet.'

'How does he pay?'

Sanjay manages to look at Wolfboy directly for a few seconds. 'He tells him things.'

'Tells who? Doctor Gregory? What sort of things?' Wolfboy kneels close to Sanjay, who winces.

'Okay, guys,' I say, unable to stand by any longer. 'Seriously, this isn't right. Sanjay's out for a good night, and we've locked him in the interrogation booth.'

'It's fine,' says Blake. 'We haven't even touched him.'

'No, it's not all right,' I tell her. 'I'm not comfortable with this. I think we should let him go.'

Wolfboy stands up. 'She's right.'

'But Sanjay is going to get us some stuff,' Blake says. 'Some institute prescription stuff. We're meeting his friend in ten minutes by the front door.'

We all look at Sanjay. His blue shirt is buttoned incorrectly and buckles in the middle.

'If we get the pills then we can find out what Paul's been taking.' Blake's eyes shine. 'We can find out if that's what's making him act strange. And find out if they're addictive. Or we could sell them to another blue person in return for more information.'

There's a sudden surge in the volume of the music. The bathroom door slams shut. Another cubicle door bangs. We hold our collective breath.

'I guess it would be useful to have the pills,' I say after a few seconds. Sanjay staggers to his feet and I grab his elbow, lending him some support.

Wolfboy helps me. 'We're not going to get you in any trouble if we do this, are we, buddy?'

Sanjay shakes his head.

'Blake, we'll keep your meeting. But then we're out of here. Twenty minutes max.'

Blake pauses and squints at Wolfboy. 'Why do you have glitter on your face?'

I stay behind while the others leave. My eyeshadow has migrated south, so I use toilet paper to tidy it up.

A girl comes out of the end cubicle and joins me at the hand basins. She has dark pixie hair and is wearing a very cool black silk playsuit. I accidentally catch her eye in the long mirror when she leans in to wash her hands.

She's extremely pretty, and familiar. What are the chances? I smear some balm on my lips.

'Is your name Ingrid?' I'm going to look royally stupid if she's not.

'Yeah,' she says, to my relief, although she doesn't seem that keen on talking to a stranger. 'Sorry, have we met before?'

'No, but I think you used to go out with a friend of mine. He's more of a friend-of-a-friend, actually. Paul?'

'Oh. Right.' She goes to the hand dryer. I can tell she'll leave as soon as her hands are dry, if not before, so I jump in quickly.

'You haven't seen him recently, like in the last few days, have you?'

'We don't really talk anymore.'

'Exes, huh? Sometimes you gotta avoid them.' I sound convincing, even though I've never managed to go out with someone for longer than three weeks.

'Yeah.' She smiles wanly. The dryer cuts out. I only have seconds.

'I wouldn't ask, it's just that my friend is really worried about him.'

That holds her attention. 'Why?'

'Do you know anything about the blue people?'

She looks me up and down.

'Please don't think I'm crazy,' I say. 'My name's Nia, and I don't normally dress this way.'

When we emerge Wolfboy is waiting at the far end of the corridor. He hasn't bothered to put his cap and glasses back on.

'What took you so long?' He spots Ingrid behind me and immediately puts his guard up.

I motion Ingrid forward, taking a split-second to appreciate how hot Wolfboy looks leaning against the wall. His shirt makes his eyes look insanely blue.

'Wolfboy, this is Ingrid. As in Paul's ex-girlfriend. Ingrid, this is Wolfboy.'

Wolfboy instantly regrets his exasperation and it's a small moment of victory for me. You can try to distract me with your kisses, sir, but I will come through with the goods in the end.

He offers his hand to Ingrid. 'It's really nice to meet you. I don't normally dress like this.'

'That's what Nia just said.' Ingrid looks from Wolfboy to me. 'Paul got more involved with the Datura people, then? Is that why you're in blue?'

'We're trying to find out more about them.'

'Wouldn't it be easier to ask him?'

'He's gone AWOL,' Wolfboy says reluctantly. 'And the last time we saw him, he wasn't particularly coherent.'

Ingrid puts her hands to her face. 'Shit. This is my fault.

I didn't want to cut him off, but he kept calling me every day, trying to get back with me.'

'It's not your fault,' I reassure her.

'After we broke up, Paul told me he had started going to the Datura Institute to take part in some research. At first I thought it sounded interesting, but after a while I didn't like the sound of all the drugs, even if they were prescribed by doctors. Paul started talking strangely about his dreams, stuff about remaking history and influencing the future.'

Wolfboy and I exchange worried looks.

'That was the last straw for me. I told him we couldn't even be friends, we couldn't have any contact.'

We leave via the main door, my eyes soaking up the soothing darkness. I take Wolfboy's hand as we cut through an open shed as massive as an airport hangar. I feel safe, even though I can barely see the ground.

'It's easier to walk in the dark with you beside me,' I tell Wolfboy, but he's lost in his own thoughts.

Blake waits for us in the laneway beyond the shed. She holds a ziplock bag containing two round tablets. They look small and innocuous.

'Well done,' I say. I want to smooth things over after telling her off about Sanjay. 'You did really well tonight, Blake.'

She beams at me. 'Wildgirl, do you think you could teach me to put on eyeshadow? Back at home?'

I try not to look too surprised. 'Sure. No problem. I've got some gold stuff that would look great on you. But I have to go home tonight. I have school tomorrow.'

'What if I won't let you go?' Wolfboy says.

'I'm pretty sure that's called kidnapping.' I keep my voice light. I pick up my teacup from where I'd hidden it.

Wolfboy makes me take a taxi home from Panwood. He and Blake pool their money to pay for it, despite my protests. The driver watches me warily in the rear-view mirror, suspicious of my blue outfit and the teacup I'm carrying. When we reach Plexus I pay him with a fistful of coins.

Even though I'm used to coming home to an empty flat, it feels different tonight. It's almost as if I live on my own, a time-travelling glimpse of being grown up and independent. I kick my shoes off and leave them in the middle of the floor among the shreds of ripped-up train ticket. I put the teacup on the windowsill, where it can get some morning sun. The plant's plump fronds glow white with a tinge of opalescent blue. I touch them gently, smiling for no one but myself. The flowers are so delicate and otherworldly. I love them.

I've been asleep for minutes, it seems, when my screeching alarm wakes me. The first thing I see is my pillow streaked with blue eyeshadow. I go into the sunny kitchen with heavy legs and a furry mouth and fill a glass with water.

I take the dregs over to the teacup on the windowsill, only to find I'm too late. The plant is already dead; its beautiful pearly leaves have turned brown and withered. Shit. My first present from Wolfboy and I've killed it in less than twelve hours.

twenty-one

Blake and I drag our feet on the way home from the border. Mist curls around our ankles as we turn into my street. When we let ourselves in I don't even look to see if there's a light on in Paul's room.

'I had an idea about what we could do with the pills,' says Blake. 'I think my friend will know what they are.'

'This friend wouldn't happen to be the Queen of the Night, would she?'

Blake nods.

'Good. We'll go see her tomorrow then. I don't have anything else to do.'

Doubt flits moth-like across Blake's face. 'I'm not sure.'

She folds the pill bag into ever-smaller squares. 'I could ask. I suppose.'

'Doesn't she like visitors? Is what she does illegal?'

'No, of course not. She has a lot of valuable equipment, and…and things, at her house. She doesn't want people to know how much she has.'

'You can tell her I can be trusted. Get some sleep, Blake. You've earned it.'

As soon as I'm alone my head starts to teem. I lie down on the couch in the front room. It's cold in here, and there are cobwebs in the corner of the ceiling, but I can't deal with the chaos of the upper floor.

Finding out what sort of pills the blue people take won't help us if we don't find Paul. The thought that I might have to email Paul's mum, who is sailing somewhere up the east coast, to tell her that her son is missing doesn't thrill me.

I close my eyes, willing myself to drift off. I want, for a few precious moments, to not exist at all.

I succeed better than I thought I would, because when I open my eyes again it's the morning. A sound has woken me. I lie still, listening. A car getting closer, then fading away. It could have been part of a dream, but I go out into the hallway to check. The corner of an envelope pokes through the mail slot.

I haven't had mail in nearly a year. There's no such

thing as a postal service in Shyness anymore.

The envelope is pale blue, without a postmark, and smaller than regulation size. My name is printed on the front in neat purple letters. I already know who it's from.

The letter is handwritten, with a familiar signature at the bottom: Dr W. Gregory. Doctor Gregory used to send me letters regularly, but I haven't had any in a while. The old letters were typed forms, with my name pasted into the greeting. This letter is more personal.

> *Dear Jethro,*
>
> *It has come to my attention that you have an interest in the workings of the Datura Institute. I'm keen to discuss my innovative programs with you, as well as several other matters of importance. Call this number to arrange a meeting: 9342 45860.*
>
> *Please pass on my kind regards to your friend Paul. I have enjoyed my recent conversations with him very much.*
>
> *Best,*
>
> *Dr W. Gregory*

A pulsing, buzzing feeling blasts away the whispery remnants of sleep. The doubt that's been eating away at my insides becomes more solid. I considered it a reprieve that Doctor Gregory didn't chase me down after Nia and I broke into Orphanville. But maybe this is how he's getting back at me.

My second impulse is to call the number. Call his bluff. And maybe he knows where Paul is. But now I'm wondering all over again if I really want to find him.

I go to Blake's room, but she's curled up under the covers, breathing heavily. We got home well after midnight, and it's only 8 a.m. now, too early to wake her. I find myself in the kitchen without knowing how I got there, pulling my phone out, dialling the number.

'Hello?' A woman's voice.

I almost hang up.

'Hello?' she repeats.

'I think I have the wrong number.'

She must put me on speaker, because her voice becomes echoey. 'You're the only person with this number,' she says.

I catch a glimpse of Orphanville as I crest the hill near my house. The towers are dark, as they have been for the last few weeks, except for the closest one, which blazes with fire. The Kidds like their bonfires, but this is bigger. Flames lick the entire top floor. A pillar of smoke climbs into the golden sky. The Panwood fire brigade won't be rushing to the scene. The late afternoon is flushed through with a warmer breeze.

It took some fast-talking with Doctor Gregory's secretary to organise a meeting place. There was no way I was going to the Datura Institute. She put me on hold several

183

times before accepting my suggestion: a dusty, unpopular cafe on O'Neira Street. Last night must have exhausted Blake, because she's been asleep all day. I didn't bother waking her. I might be able to get more information on my own from Doctor Gregory before we go see the Queen of the Night.

A gaudy, flashing Mother Mary looks down benevolently on me at the entrance to the building. I cross myself automatically, the habit of too many years of Catholic schooling. The owner of the cafe has an obsession with Mexican Day of the Dead paraphernalia. Skeleton statues lurk in every crevice of the main passageway. I walk through to the main room, which is as quiet as a crypt.

Doctor Gregory has already arrived. He sits in a sunken square pit with benches all around and a lace-draped table in the middle. A man at supreme ease. The very sight causes a nasty taste in my mouth. I don't even want to be in the same room as him.

He makes to stand up and shake my hand.

'Don't bother,' I say, and sit on the other side of the table, as far away as I can get. Doctor Gregory is dressed for business, in a white shirt, striped tie and suit pants. Everything about him is glossy and fake—from his tan to the hefty watch on his wrist. I check the corners of the room. A suited bodyguard stands next to the bar. Of course he didn't come on his own. I suppose the fact that he didn't bring a small army is a good sign that I'm not about to be kidnapped.

'Jethro, it's a pleasure to see you again.'

The way he says my name makes me realise he already thinks he's won by getting me to meet him.

'Spare me.' I shift on the hard bench. I deliberately wore my oldest jeans and a ripped flannie. 'What's this about?'

A waiter deposits a tray of drinks on our table. Doctor Gregory waits until he leaves before speaking.

'We might have to work on your manners,' he says, plucking a cigarette from a pack on the table. 'You're a touch savage, I must say. Do you have a light?'

I shake my head, refusing to play along. Doctor Gregory shrugs and finds his own lighter in his pocket. He places two shot glasses in front of me, and two in front of him.

'You've been asking about my dream program.'

'That's right.'

'Do you want to participate?' A mocking smile creeps onto his orange face. Smoke unfurls from his mouth.

'No. I want to know why Paul is treated differently from your other patients.'

That makes him raise his eyebrows.

'You have done your research,' he says with fatherly approval. He raises his glass with his spare hand. 'Paul is a special case. Cheers.'

I move the glasses away from me. 'Special how?'

'Half of the participants in my dream program are insomniacs. It's ironic, isn't it? Being surrounded by night, yet finding sleep elusive?' Doctor Gregory smiles without showing his teeth. 'Their dreams are nothing to them, so they give them to me readily in return for a few hours of oblivion. Following an extremely strict pharmaceutical protocol, I might add. Then there are the patients who are addicted to dreaming, Dreamers of the most dedicated kind. Our medications are ten times cleaner than what they can buy on the street. We negotiate taking a portion of their dreams, and they keep some for their own recreation.'

Doctor Gregory pauses to alternate sips from his remaining glass, and draws from his cigarette. His thin dry lips make me feel sick. I notice he also talks as if dreams were objects, commodities, capable of transaction.

'Your dear friend Paul, however, is different. Paul has no interest in sharing his dreams with anyone. Which is not to say I haven't taken a small peek occasionally. Clinical interest, you understand. Most fascinating. Paul is unhealthily fixated on the past. He wants to cycle through the same events, again and again. He has little interest in exploring the stranger horizons of nocturnal travel. You know, parallel universes, prophecy, and the like.'

I decide to humour him and pretend that he's bottling dreams like Sanjay said.

'What do you do with their dreams? You go to so much

effort, you must really need them.'

'Well, thank you for asking me that, Jethro.' Doctor Gregory attempts to smile, but it comes out more like a grimace. 'Dreams are windows onto people's desires—desires they try to keep secret, or even desires they didn't know they had. And if you know a man's desires, then you can make him do anything.'

I have to stop myself from jiggling my legs. He's told me nothing concrete. 'Why do you need to make people do what you want them to? Aren't you too old to be playing with dolls?'

Another sip, another draw.

'Reasons, reasons. The one thing humans have in common is that they are all searching for answers.' He stubs his cigarette in an ashtray. 'Except for our Paul; he thinks all we need is *love*.'

I feign standing up to leave.

Doctor Gregory slaps both hands on the table. Gold rings line up across his knuckles. 'I don't discuss my work with many people, Jethro. Only those who can grasp it.'

'You think I'm dumb enough to fall for your false flattery?' I sit back down despite my words.

'You've matured recently, Jethro. Changed. I can see that. I get the feeling you regard me as an enemy. I've searched my conscience for a likely reason. That business with the Kidds? That was nothing. I don't particularly care if you visit Orphanville. I don't particularly care if you pick fights with people in my employ. I was already planning on scaling back the Kidds' activity. You even did me a favour when you released the tarsier. Doesn't that make you think some of our interests might be the same? That we could work together?'

I would never stoop that low, but I see an opportunity. 'You can start by telling me why you've targeted Paul. If he doesn't give you his dreams, what do you get out of it?' I try not to make it obvious that I'm holding my breath.

'I thought you would have figured that out by now, Jethro. I give Paul the necessary pills to put him in his perfect dream universe, and he gives me information about you.'

I blink. Everything flashes white for a few seconds. Then I'm back in the room.

'He wouldn't do that.' I regret my words immediately.

Doctor Gregory smiles more successfully this time. With teeth. His eyes are two coal-black voids. Empty eyes. 'It's never nice to admit that we don't know our friends as well as we thought we did.'

I grip the edge of the seat. Paul betraying me. This is the rotting dark possibility that has been sitting in my stomach.

'Tell me where he is.' I can barely get the words out. Doctor Gregory looks genuinely surprised. He's a hammy actor so I can tell the difference.

'I don't know where Paul is. Maybe you've scared him into hiding. If it makes you feel any better, he was initially very reluctant to tell me anything. But once he became more dependent on his cherished dream state, he was far more obliging.'

'There's nothing to tell,' I say. My fingers are cramping.

'You'd be surprised what I can do with the smallest detail.'

I let go of the seat. Flight seems the most useful response right now. That, or smashing the slimy look of concern off Doctor Gregory's face.

'You can't mess with people's lives like this. It's wrong.'

'Shyness is a unique environment, Jethro. A battlefield in one way, a petri dish in another. Some of us are better equipped to take advantage of this. Some of us are better equipped to make sense of the phenomena that surround us. Why are you so resistant to embracing the possibilities?'

He lights another cigarette and blows smoke at the ceiling. I don't know what to say. I'll never come out of a conversation with Doctor Gregory on top because he manipulates words better than I ever could. But a few of his words stick, and I realise he needs Shyness more than it needs him. I pull Delilah's book from my pocket.

'I've been doing some light reading in my spare time.' I hold the book up so he can read the cover. 'Are you familiar with this particular branch of the family tree?'

For a microsecond, Doctor Gregory's mask slips. It gives me courage to keep talking.

'You'll be screwed if someone upsets your petri dish. If what this book says is true, things won't stay the same in Shyness forever. Are you really going to sit there and pretend you haven't noticed the changes around here?'

His face hardens. 'I make the changes.'

'Yeah, you keep telling yourself that.'

'You can't decide if you feel unique or alone, Jethro, but I have others like you in my care. Yours is not the most severe case I've seen, not by a long shot. It really is so very fascinating to watch the battle of nature and civilisation up close.'

I stand up, tuck the book away again.

'But you're not the only person I have my eye on,' he continues. 'That Diana, she's a special little girl, isn't she?'

I'm by his side in a flash, grabbing him by the shirt, hauling him up off the seat. Doctor Gregory's face is abstract. Terracotta-coloured. A collection of shapes and lines. The bodyguard moves into my peripheral vision, a blurry dark figure, but Doctor Gregory shakes his head.

I pull my fist back, cocked, ready to strike.

'I'm winning the battle,' I say. I let him go. He falls onto the seat, breathing heavily. I jump out of the pit and head for the door.

twenty-two

There's only one place I can think to go. I slow to a walk on the steep path up to the lip of the volcano. There are no lights, crowd, noise. I don't know what else I was expecting. It's not fight night, after all.

But when I reach the top and look down onto the cycling track, I see that I haven't wasted my time. A small light burns at the centre of the basin. There are three people in the cage.

The Gentleman sees me coming and pushes open a gate on the side of the cage, his eyes friendly in his dust-streaked face. I duck through and he bolts the door behind me. He pulls me into a strange, fleeting embrace, and I feel the strength of his arms, his bigness and wildness. Clad in nothing but a pair of stubbies, every inch of his skin, from collarbone to toes, is covered in thick coarse hair.

'Wolfboy,' is all he says, as if I drop in every day.

I nod, suddenly shy.

The cage is lit only by two heavy-duty torches placed on the ground in a crisscross arrangement. I don't recognise the other two men in the ring. They don't hide their curiosity. The smell of sweat and dust is strong.

'Paddy.'

The Gentleman flicks his hand, and a man steps forward. He's older than the Gentleman, short and squat and wearing a faded tracksuit. Sleek black hair grows from his eyebrow line, all the way over the top of his head and down the back of his neck. A thick glossy pelt.

'Better take your shoes off.' The Gentleman leans against the cage wall.

I drop my eyes to Paddy's bare feet. He has ugly knobbly toes but his feet are ordinary.

I realise I've come here to fight.

I kick off my shoes and step into the centre of the cross-hatched light. Paddy bows. I return the gesture.

We circle each other on the dirt, our feet kicking up puffs of dust. I watch Paddy. Soon the world is reduced to the two of us, staring, orbiting.

An unexpected calm descends over me. I can feel

everything: the dirt between my toes, the barest wind on my skin, my fingers curling into fists.

And then Paddy charges, planting a shoulder in my stomach.

I take the blow, letting myself buckle at the middle and fall. My back slams against the ground and I kick up into the air. A moment later I'm back on my feet.

Paddy cricks his neck to the side. I throw myself at him. I grab him around the middle and hurl him to the other side of the cage. He hits the ground, then comes at me on all fours, crawling fast. Blood trickles from the corner of his mouth. He grabs my ankles. I kick frantically until I free a foot, stomp hard between his shoulderblades, leaving a streak of dirt on his tracksuit.

Paddy grunts and collapses but he still manages to topple me by pulling my ankle.

I smack into the ground, a skyscraper under demolition. My chest heaves, trying to suck in air. I finally kick free, and launch myself at him again. I'm getting tired and my heart is beating out of time. Paddy and I roll over and over until I lose sense of which way is up.

He gets a punch in to the side of my head and there are stars everywhere. When my vision clears I'm sitting on his chest, pinning his arms above his head.

Paddy taps the ground—'I'm out!'—and I let go.

I get to my feet straightaway, but the ground tilts under

me. Paddy rolls away. The Gentleman pushes off the cage wall, clapping. He collars my waist when my legs give way, and helps me to a sitting position on the ground.

I tip my head to look at the stars through the cage. They're pulsating with disco light. I might feel fantastic, I'm not sure.

Seconds later I'm positive I'm going to throw up. I put my head between my knees until the nausea passes. When I look up, the Gentleman is watching me without concern.

'You're punch drunk,' he says. 'It'll pass quickly. Come with me to the clubhouse.'

The clubhouse is a long narrow shed with a concrete floor and a corrugated iron roof. It's littered with mattresses and blankets, kerosene lamps and rusty gym equipment.

A bruise is blooming on my cheekbone. Paddy hasn't fared any better, but he still shakes my hand, and then sinks onto a camp bed with a groan.

I wince when I lower myself onto a bench.

The Gentleman grabs a bottle of whisky and offers it to me. I refuse, but he insists. 'Trust me.'

The spirit burns in my mouth.

'Feel better?' he asks.

I shrug. What an unanswerable question.

'I'm not going to be able to convince you to fight for stakes, am I?' he asks.

'Probably not.'

He doesn't seem too fazed by that. He draws from the bottle, swills the liquid.

'So you know, people here come and go as they please. No rules, no pressure. If you want to train with us, spar with us, anytime, you're always welcome.'

'Good to know.'

I take another sip from the bottle, but it makes my nausea well up again. My insides are hot and loose.

'What have you been doing tonight, Jethro?'

I think of Doctor Gregory's words, the smooth veneer that does little to cover the sick reality. I look at the Gentleman, barely clothed and unwashed and straight out of the Wild West, and I trust him implicitly.

'I've been wondering about Night Sickness,' I say.

'What's that?'

'It's this.' I point to myself. 'It's being different.'

The Gentleman baulks. 'This isn't an illness, Jethro. It's a gift, a privilege. Who called it a sickness?'

'Something I read.'

'Something you read in Doctor Gregory's pamphlets? I already told you he's a quack. D'you know when I first set up this place, when I first started the fights, he came calling? He pretended he was talking to me man-to-man, but he made it very clear that he was doing me a favour by considering me an equal. He wanted to do a deal. He offered me money for access to my fighters.'

'What did he want with them?'

'That was never on the table.' The Gentleman puts the whisky bottle on the ground next to his feet. 'One reason to distrust him. Second reason, the way he talked, he thought we needed tempering, controlling. He talked of a cure, of all things.'

The Gentleman's smile is devilishly white. 'Every one of those ordinary yokel Locals that come to my fights on a Sunday night, who throw their hard-earned cash at my fighters, they want to be us. They envy us. We are part of the night. More than they are, and they know it. The night makes us. I don't need Doctor Gregory's money, and I don't want a cure.'

I blink, freeing myself of the Gentleman's considerable charisma. I like him, but I don't want to be like him. So where does that leave me? My confusion must be evident, because the Gentleman leans over and grabs my left bicep. I do my best not to wince.

'This here is your anger, Jethro.' He switches to my right arm. 'And this is your sadness. This *is* your strength; this is what makes you different.' He releases me. 'I know you're not looking for advice, but I will give it regardless. Don't try to control it, don't hold it in, let it be what it is. You're fine as you are, Jethro.'

I don't run on the way home, I walk. I cross over the creek and skirt Orphanville. I desperately want to drop in on Diana and Ortie, to sit with them while they eat dinner on the big studio table, but I can't let them see my tenderised face. And I'm not sure I'd be able to stop myself from telling Ortolan what Doctor Gregory said about Diana. I know he's all hot air, but Ortolan doesn't.

I settle for calling their landline, as I flirt with the edges of Shyness and Panwood all the way along Grey Street. There's no answer so I peel away from the main road, heading for home.

23

I've barely exited the school gates when my phone rings. A private number.

'Hola?' I say. I had Spanish sixth period and I'm still in the zone.

'Wildgirl, is that you? It's Blake.'

Blake talks as if she's scared of the phone.

'Hi, honey, how are you going?'

There's a pause. I keep walking towards the main road. Blake's next words gush forth in a rush.

'Wolfboy won't answer his phone and I don't know where he is and I didn't know who else to call.'

'What's wrong?'

'It's Paul. He's home. Or I found him. I need you to come.'

I'm silent, wondering how Blake can't figure out I'm probably the last person Paul wants to see.

'Wildgirl, he won't wake up.'

Blake's face floats pale and worried at the front door. She cracks it open a bare inch, until she sees it's me. I'm shivering after the abrupt transformation from day to night. Even with a jumper on, my summer school dress is too flimsy. 'Where is he?'

'In here.' Blake pulls me into the front room. 'The power's out and I need to find candles, but I don't want to leave him.'

Paul lies on the floor next to the couch, covered in a tartan blanket. The dark room could be a funeral parlour, and Paul could be a corpse laid out for viewing. His eyes are closed, his face blank.

'He's warm, and his pulse seems fine.' Blake kneels beside him and holds his hand. She's calmer than I was expecting her to be.

I put my hand on Paul's scrawny chest, feeling it rise and fall. His resemblance to a corpse diminishes when I touch him.

'Tell me what happened.'

'I don't know. I was asleep and when I woke up, no one was home. I made myself cornflakes and listened to some music. I could smell smoke, so I went outside to check.

Paul was lying on the doorstep. I don't know how long he'd been there for. He could have been there for hours.'

Blake tucks her hair behind her ears. Her face is tight. I feel sorry for her finding Paul on her own.

'I dragged him in here. At first I tried to carry him, but he was too heavy. That's how I know he won't wake up. It took me ages, and I accidentally banged him into the door and he still didn't wake up.'

'You did well to get him this far. Let's lift him onto the couch.'

Blake takes Paul's feet and I grab under his shoulders. Together we get him onto the couch. Paul's breathing doesn't alter, and he doesn't flinch when we move him. He really is fast asleep.

'What do you think is wrong with him? Why won't he wake up?' Blake asks.

'I don't know.' Paul's expression is so peaceful compared to the last time I saw him. Only his eyes move, flicking from side to side beneath the lids. I point them out to Blake.

'That's what happens when you dream.' I dredge up what we learned in Psychology last year, glad to have something concrete to grab on to. 'It's called rapid eye movement. REM. It's the phase of sleep where you're most likely to dream.'

We watch Paul's eyeballs slide for a moment.

'Do you think he overdosed on dreaming drugs?'

'Possibly. It's the likeliest explanation.' I wonder how long he's been in this state. I try to calculate the logistics of getting him to a hospital. Other than not waking up, though, he seems okay. 'Maybe this is normal. Maybe when the blue people dream they get in a really deep sleep.'

Maybe I'm talking out of my arse. Blake looks as dubious as I feel.

I try to think logically. 'Okay, this is the plan. We keep calling Wolfboy until he picks up. We watch Paul. Every half an hour we check his pulse and temperature.'

'There's a first aid kit under the kitchen sink, with a thermometer,' says Blake. 'That's where the candles are as well.'

I fetch the candles from the kitchen, sparking one before I head back. The front door clicks as I reach the top of the hallway. I don't even have enough time to tense up before the door opens.

'You look like a ghost,' Wolfboy says. He rushes towards me and sweeps me up in a big bear hug.

'Candle! Candle!' I try to keep the flame from singeing my hair. The first aid kit falls to the floor. He releases me and kisses me gently on the lips. I get a closer look at him; there's a definite sunset-coloured bruise on the side of his face.

'Are you okay?' I pat my fingers over his cheekbone.

'What happened? Did you get into a fight? Was it Doctor Gregory?'

'Stop asking questions for a second, Nia, and I might be able to answer. I'm fine. I'm so glad you're here.'

'Where have you been? Blake's been calling you.'

He kisses me again, everything about him big and warm and strong. 'I went to boxing practice,' he says incongruously, in between bombing my cheek and neck with light kisses. 'What are you doing here so soon? I thought you were going to call me after school.'

'Don't panic.'

I lead him into the front room, in time to see Blake prising Paul's eyelids open.

'What's going on in there?' she asks loudly.

I'd laugh at her unscientific methods if I didn't see Wolfboy's face pale. He joins Blake at Paul's side, searches Paul's pockets, then pinches the inside of his arm, hard. I spill wax on the coffee table and stand the candle up. Blake fills Wolfboy in.

'This could be what happens when you take those pills,' she finishes. 'He could be fine in an hour.'

She doesn't look as if she really believes that. I didn't even believe it when I said almost the same thing to her.

'If he's so fine, then why would someone dump him anonymously on the doorstep?' Wolfboy looks down at Paul, his expression odd. I lean against the sideboard, keeping my distance. I'm out of my depth. This is so much worse than holding a friend's hair back while they puke up half a bottle of vodka. I would know what to do if this happened at home. The choices would be obvious. But this is Shyness. There's been no talk of doctors or police.

Wolfboy rubs his eyes. 'I don't know if I can be bothered getting him out of this mess.'

'You don't mean that,' I say. Blake looks quietly outraged.

'You're right. I should have chased him the other night,' Wolfboy says. 'I should have kept him in the house and not let him out of my sight.'

He looks at Blake. 'Can your friend help us? The Queen? Is this the sort of thing she can fix?'

Blake squirms, scuffs her sneaker. 'When I found him, I wanted to call her right away. But I didn't want to make you mad.'

'Who's this?' I ask.

'Why would I be mad? I've been trying to—' Wolfboy catches himself, clearly exasperated. 'We don't have time for this. So, the Queen is a nurse, or is she…?'

'Not exactly,' says Blake.

I clap my hands to my face. 'Are we taking Paul to a *witch doctor*?'

~

In Shyness, I only have half a grasp on where everything is located. But I know for a fact that I haven't been anywhere near this place before.

The flat silhouettes of trees gather close before us. Or wannabe trees. An entire forest of them, cutout trees that look like they've been steamrolled flat. Uniform black and plain wood, large and small. Some with saw-toothed outlines, others with exaggerated bubbleheads. The forest looks like an unfinished film set, or a fledgling dream.

I'm so busy gawking Blake and Wolfboy almost slip from sight. Wolfboy hunches over, pushing Paul in a rusty wheelbarrow. Blake walks ahead, sure-footed, picking her path through the trees. My feet kick up a flurry of wood shavings. As enchanting as it is, I wouldn't want to be alone in this labyrinth.

'Can I get this straight,' I say when I catch them. 'There's a queen of Shyness that no one thought to tell me about? And she's also a witch doctor?'

This makes Blake and even Wolfboy smile, despite the seriousness of our situation. Sometimes they're so annoyingly oblivious to how strange their suburb is.

'The Queen of the Night is an expert,' Blake says. 'If anyone will know what to do with Paul, she will.'

'What qualifications does she have?'

'That's not really the point,' says Blake.

I cross my arms over my chest, a hair's breadth away

from petulance. 'These woods are full of eyes,' I say, instead of defending my right to ask normal, rational questions. 'I feel like someone is watching us.'

'Don't worry. We're nearly there.'

Beyond the edge of the forest is a strip of vacant land, a ditch, and then another normal residential street. I scan the footpaths for pedestrians. No one. The eyes haven't followed us. Paul's arms and legs dangle over the sides of the wheelbarrow, barely clearing the road. Surely what we're doing is weird, even by Shyness standards.

Blake stops on the next corner, outside an old-fashioned apartment building with curved balconies.

'This is it.'

The building is in pretty good nick, but it definitely isn't a palace fit for a queen. It's not even a falling-down gothic mansion. I glance up. Three storeys of red brick. Elegant metal letters sit above the ground floor windows: *WOOKEY & SALAMON*. A smudge of black flits across a balcony and out of sight, sending a skittery shiver travelling up my spine.

Blake opens a wrought-iron door that leads to a chilly vestibule. The steps are too much of a challenge for the rickety wheelbarrow. Wolfboy is forced to heave Paul over his shoulder, fireman-style.

We move forward into the dark building. 'What's that smell?' Wolfboy's voice echoes. We must be in a large space. I sniff but I can't smell anything.

'Keep moving forward,' calls out Blake, 'and stay close to the sides.'

When my eyes adjust I realise that the entire ground floor is an open space. There are no lights or lamps or candles in here, but despite that the ground is glowing green.

'Dirt,' says Wolfboy. 'That's what I smelt. It's a room full of dirt.'

I crouch where the glow is strongest. A peaty smell fills my nostrils. Hazy green shapes become miniature umbrellas and round buttons.

'This is strange,' I say to Wolfboy in a low voice. 'Is this what you were expecting?'

'I don't know what to expect.' Wolfboy shifts Paul on his shoulder with a grunt. Paul's arms hang limply.

'We're late.' Blake sounds impatient, already on the other side of the room. I can see now that there are narrow concrete edges around the pit of dirt. 'I said we'd be here ten minutes ago. She hates it when people are late.'

'You try carrying a dead weight on your own,' says Wolfboy, but Blake has already disappeared up a flight of stairs lit with candles.

'Do you want some help?'

'He's not that heavy. There are a few advantages to being an animal,' Wolfboy grunts, climbing the stairs.

I whack him one. 'You're not an animal any more than I'm a fairy. Stop being so angsty.'

At the top of the staircase is a door with a frosted window engraved with a *W&S*. Blake waits for us on the landing.

'What's growing down there?' I ask her.

'Luminescent fungi. Foxfire and Jack O'Lanterns mostly.'

I file that info under Strange Trivia. Blake knocks on the door, turning to give us an excited smile. Personally I wish I were meeting the Queen in something a little more glamorous than my school dress.

'Come in,' I hear a female voice say.

24

We follow Blake into a room that looks like a cross between an office and someone's house.

'Put him down here,' says the Queen to Wolfboy, patting a desk. Wolfboy lays Paul carefully down on the flat surface, and the Queen fetches a cushion to lay under his head.

The Queen of the Night is not at all what I expected.

She's my age, plump, with dyed black hair, blue eyes, red lipstick and a pretty freckled face.

'You can call me Amelia,' she says to me and Wolfboy. 'Take a seat where you can find it.'

Amelia's apartment is large and, though clean, it's filled

with enough furniture for four families. There are framed pictures on the walls, and wooden cabinets with hundreds of tiny drawers, and an entire six-person dining setting pushed into a corner. Wolfboy sits in a leather armchair with burst seams, and I perch on the armrest. He rests his arm across my leg, and trails his fingers up and down my calf. I try to think serious thoughts.

Amelia leans over Paul and checks most of the things we've already covered. Blake must have told her a lot on the phone, because she seems unsurprised by his condition. Paul's eyes are still now, and his face is smooth and pale. He has a wide mouth and eyelashes long enough to cast feathery shadows on his cheeks. He's actually quite pretty, the perfect halfway point between Anglo and Korean.

Blake peers around Amelia's shoulder. 'He looks like Sleeping Beauty.'

'Don't ever say that to his face,' says Wolfboy. 'Actually, do. If he wakes up, promise me you'll say that to his face.'

Blake scowls. 'I'm not going to say that. And it's not *if* he wakes up, it's *when*. Right, Meels?'

Amelia takes off Paul's shoes and socks and tickles his feet. He doesn't move. She lifts his arm into the air, and lets it drop. Her manner is unhurried and her movements practised. From where I'm sitting it's clear she's a professional. Even if I don't know exactly what sort of professional.

'So, uh, Amelia, are you Wookey or Salamon?' asks Wolfboy.

I grab his hand and hold it still. I want to concentrate.

'Neither. My grandfather on my mother's side was a Wookey.' While Amelia talks she goes to a cupboard and selects a small bottle from the dozens inside. She uncorks it and waves it under Paul's nostrils. Blake follows her every move, watching and learning. I'm surprised she doesn't have her notebook out.

'Grandpa used to own this building. After he died, my parents divided it up into apartments. We lived in this one and leased the rest out. When the renters and my parents left Shyness, I ripped down the dividers on the bottom floor, fixed up the rooftop and turned it back into the family business. I had to make adjustments because of the Darkness, but I did it in the end.'

Amelia corks the bottle.

'So what is the family business?'

Amelia fixes Wolfboy with a no-nonsense look. 'It's the business of helping you, I presume.'

I squash my smile. I can already see why Amelia is nicknamed the Queen. She turns to Blake. 'B, did you bring the pills with you?'

Blake fishes the ziplock bag out of her pocket.

'Standard sleep program medication.' Amelia points to the pale blue pill. 'This puts the patient in an extremely deep dream state. The orange pill enables them to dream lucidly.'

'What does that mean?' I ask.

'It means you know that you're dreaming while you're doing it, and you can remember your dreams when you wake up. But it's also rumoured this second pill makes it possible for a third party to observe, possibly even extract or record the dream.'

'And you believe that?' Wolfboy sounds about as incredulous as I feel. Then again, what Amelia said correlates with Sanjay's babble.

'It's theoretically feasible. I think Doctor Gregory has the tools to observe dreams, and possibly influence them in minor ways. I don't imagine he can do more than that. The rest is spin.' Amelia frowns. She seems troubled by the contents of the bag. Her voice trails off as she wanders over to a filing cabinet and fetches some digital scales. The scales beep when they're turned on. She places the bag on the tray. 'I'd be interested in analysing these in detail, but we need them, and we don't have time.'

'Do you think Paul overdosed on this stuff?' Wolfboy's hand tightens on my knee.

'I think he's taken the medication too often, without enough of a break in between dreams. He wouldn't be the only person. I saw someone else with the same problem last month.'

I think of Paul's twitching eyes from earlier. Even from here I can see that they've started to move again. 'Could he be stuck in a dream?'

Amelia looks at me approvingly. 'I think that's exactly what's happening. How long ago did you find him?'

'About three hours ago,' says Blake, 'but he was already asleep when I found him, so we don't know how long he's been this way.' That makes Amelia frown.

'If he doesn't wake by tomorrow, we need to go in and drag him out.'

'How will we do that?' Wolfboy sounds even more sceptical now. I don't blame him.

'It will be easier if I show you upstairs. Come.'

At first I think the staircase leads to another floor, but then I realise that I'm looking at black sky and stars instead of a ceiling. The room has walls but no roof. The walls are lined with metal shelves crowded with pots. All around us are the monstery silhouettes of plants, their leaves flashing silver in the moonlight.

I home in on an old margarine tub containing a familiar white plant.

'This is the same as my teacup plant, isn't it?' I ask Blake.

She nods. 'Indian Pipe. One of the few plants in the whole world that doesn't need any sunlight to survive.'

My plant didn't stand a chance in sunny Plexus. I don't want Blake or Wolfboy to find out I've already killed it. 'What's your favourite?'

Blake drags me to another shelf. 'This one—a Bat Plant. Isn't it creepy?'

The Bat Plant's leaves are bat-wing-shaped, with hairy trailing tendrils. At the plant's centre is a twisted black flower like a shrivelled face.

'Yech.' I'm not brave enough to lean closer. The flower might come to life and bite me. I turn to get Wolfboy's attention, but he is nowhere among the shelves. Amelia has disappeared too.

'Up here.'

Wolfboy stands on top of the far wall, the moon sitting on his shoulder, the star-scattered sky surrounding him. My breath catches. He looks at ease on the high wall, at least four metres above the floor, a ladder resting at his feet. I half expect him to throw his head back and howl, like he did when we first met.

'This way,' he says.

I touch the ladder and look up. The rungs are solid under my hands but it's a long way up. Wolfboy kneels and holds out his hand. 'A rung at a time, that's all. Eyes on me.'

When I crawl over the lip of the wall I'm relieved to see there's no corresponding drop on the other side, only the large flat rooftop of the apartment building. I spy a greenhouse in the corner, and literally hundreds of plants on wheeled gurneys lining the edges of the roof, and crammed around chimneys and air ducts. Amelia is still nowhere in sight.

'Wow.'

I've never really thought about it before, but there's not much in the way of successful gardens in Shyness, at least not as far as I've seen. The Memorial Gardens is a graveyard of fallen trees; lawns and nature strips are nonexistent, and the creek is choked with dead foliage. And yet here, miraculously, is a rooftop jungle growing in the dark.

Blake pulls herself over the wall and skips ahead of us. 'Do you love it?'

I do love it, but I'm even more confused than ever. I catch Wolfboy's eye and he seems similarly bemused. I try to think up ways a crack gardener could help Paul. The rooftop looks as if it's organised into plant types, in the way a botanic garden might be. One corner is devoted to cactus-like plants; a row of low glass boxes is home to a group of anaemic flowers. In the centre is something else familiar. I pull Wolfboy towards it, ducking under a vine with purple fruit.

It's growing in a rusted bathtub with clawed feet, a fairly ordinary tree, except for the dozens of cream trumpet-shaped flowers crowding its branches. The flowers have delicate frilled edges, and hang face-down, like petticoats hung out to dry.

'Datura,' I say.

Wolfboy plucks a flower and examines it. 'Are you sure?'

'Yeah. Look at it. Exactly like the drawing.' Its scent is so strong my head spins. 'It doesn't look poisonous, does it? It's too beautiful for that.'

'Why would Amelia grow datura?'

'I don't know. It shouldn't be able to grow in the dark either.'

'Over here!' Blake beckons from the door of the greenhouse, practically jumping up and down.

I smile at her. 'She's in her element, isn't she? How did she meet Amelia?'

Wolfboy drops the flower on the concrete. 'No idea. They're not the likeliest of pals, are they?'

I pick a path through the pots. 'Do you think Blake wants to be a gardener or something?'

'She's interested in everything about nature. She could be a zoologist or botanist or biologist.' Wolfboy nearly trips on a coiled garden hose. 'Except she hasn't been to school in years. Even Paul and Thom and I left before finishing. We've probably all screwed up our prospects.'

Amelia ushers us inside the greenhouse.

The air in the glass shed is warm and humid. We huddle in the only space that isn't occupied by a trolley. Scant moonlight makes it through the dusty glass. There are four industrial lamps with large metal sunflower heads, but they aren't switched on.

'So the family business is a nursery?' asks Wolfboy.

Amelia ignores his question. 'If you want to meet the real Queen of the Night,' she says, squatting low and patting an enormous glazed pot sitting on a pallet, 'then here she is. The night-blooming cereus.'

We all look at the plant, which looks like a stringy and not-very-healthy cactus. It has several tightly closed buds scattered along its dry arms. Blake dotes over it.

Amelia sighs. 'I thought she was getting close.' She flicks on a lamp and trains its warm yellow glow on a group of plants. Only when she's done this does she address Wolfboy.

'I don't run a nursery. I'm a herbalist. My grandfather did this, and his father, and his father before him, although they preferred to call themselves wildcrafters back then. I have all their notes and books and case studies, passed down through generations. We don't just prescribe and use plants, we grow them. Every plant on this rooftop has a purpose. Each has properties that can help or harm humans. My job is to grow and propagate them, then prepare them for use.'

'You can make us a medicine that will wake Paul up,

can't you?' says Blake. It's clear from the way she looks at Amelia that she thinks she can do anything—even drive away the Darkness with a single leaf, if she wanted to.

'No, I can't do that.'

'Oh,' says Blake.

'What I can offer you is—less straightforward than that. The pills that Paul took are derived from naturally occurring plant substances. I have those plants growing in this garden. I suggest we send someone into Paul's dream to talk him out again. Coax him back.'

There's silence. Somewhere in the greenhouse, water drips. I want to laugh, but no one else is laughing.

Blake breaks the silence. 'Of course…' she says, like it's the most obvious solution in the world.

I wait for Wolfboy to speak up, but he doesn't. Someone has to say something.

'What do you mean, send someone into his dream?' I ask.

'Exactly how it sounds.' I can't see Amelia's face properly with the lamp blasting behind her. 'I'll use the plants to make a preparation that allows the user to penetrate the subconscious. Not just their own, but that of others near them. We'll give a dose to Paul, and a dose to one of you.'

'Bags not me,' says Blake.

'I'll do it.' Wolfboy is unhesitating.

'Whoever takes the solution will also take the blue pill

to induce a deep sleep. The combination of the two will give the ability to enter Paul's dreams.'

I frown. 'How many times have you done this before?'

'I've never had to. Usually the sleeper wakes up before it's necessary. But I've tried these plant extracts on myself, and they do what I say they do. I need twenty-four hours to prepare, and it's a full moon tomorrow. That's good timing. In the meantime, you can cross your fingers that Paul wakes up first.'

'Okay, then,' says Wolfboy, as if it's all decided. I'm already composing a lecture to deliver in private; I don't want to parade my doubts in front of Amelia and Blake.

'Queen?' Blake's voice squeaks. 'Meels? I think it's happening.'

Amelia waves us in closer. While we've been talking, one of the buds on the Queen of the Night has raised its head and started to open. Thin outer petals unfurl after their long sleep. Inside the bud are paler white petals fluttering to life. The heart of the flower seems to glow with a pure light. Soon, the flower is the size of a human hand, and opening more each minute. The baby petals in the very centre are pink.

Blake looks up at us, her face luminous and full of awe.

Amelia uses a pair of tweezers to remove a pink central petal and drop it into a jar. 'Good,' she says. 'Now we can collect the rest of what we need.'

twenty-five

'Should I leave these here?' I stand in the kitchen doorway with the empty pizza boxes and point at the rubbish bin.

Amelia is in the process of crushing spidery roots under a large blade and tipping them into a saucepan. There are jars and packets littering the counter.

'You can wedge them between the bin and the cupboard.'

'I could take them downstairs. Find a dumpster or someone else's bin.'

'That won't be necessary. I've got an incinerator on the roof.' Amelia's steel-capped boots clip the linoleum. She places the saucepan on the stove, next to two other bubbling pans. Condensation mists on the kitchen windows. The air is pungent and medicinal.

On the other bench Blake works in a cloud of flour. Her fingers are webbed with sticky dough. Blake and Amelia look at home in the small kitchen, as if they do this all the time.

'So, you've met my niece?' I ease my phone out of my pocket. No messages. I texted Ortie earlier but she still hasn't replied.

'Diana?' Amelia glances up fleetingly. 'What a sweetie she is.'

'She helped us put those tin cans and cups all over the streets,' Blake chimes in.

I pick up a brown paper packet. It looks similar to the ones that Lupe was carrying in her handbag that night we first saw the blue people.

'Don't touch that,' says Amelia, and I drop it immediately. It's clear there's no place for me in this kitchen. 'Wildgirl's waiting for you in the guest room. The flowers gave her hay fever so we told her to lie down.'

'I don't mind taking first shift watching Paul,' I say.

'He's stable,' Amelia says. 'Blake and I can manage it between us. Besides, you two can barely keep your hands off each other. You're better off leaving it to those who aren't distracted.'

Blake snorts, then when she catches me staring daggers

at her becomes very interested in drying her hands on her apron. Amelia, however, stares at me calmly while my face heats up. I have a paranoid moment where I think she knows everything about me. I want to defend my professionalism, not to mention my serious concerns about Paul, but all I can think is: there are too many girls in this building. I'm outnumbered three to one.

Amelia uses a knife to gesture at the top of the refrigerator. 'Take those with you. Wildgirl wanted something to sleep in.'

I gather the pile of clothes in my arms and hesitate at the threshold, still thinking of the brown packets.

'Do you sell tea to Guadalupe?'

Amelia's face brightens. 'Yes. I make a special brew exclusively for her. I didn't realise you knew her.'

I nod, and turn to go.

'Wolfboy,' says Amelia. 'Don't worry about Paul. We need you rested for tomorrow. It's getting late. So relax, and sleep.'

The residential wing unfolds down a long corridor lined with faded red wallpaper. A door is ajar halfway down, spilling a shard of light across the carpet. The guest room.

Nia sits cross-legged in the middle of a four-poster bed, swamped by the hanging canopy and the brocade bedspread and dozens of cushions.

'Crazy set-up, huh?' She sneezes violently.

I place the pyjamas on the end of the bed and sit down. Nia grabs a handful of tissues from the box on the bedside table. A mammoth gilt-edged mirror runs parallel to the bed. All the furniture is antique.

'It smells a bit musty in here, I know, but the bed linen is clean. I checked.' Nia blows her nose loudly. 'I wish I had my antihistamines with me. I wish I had a lot of things with me. My toothbrush. A change of clothes. Socks.'

'I brought you pyjamas.' I shift further up the bed. The mattress is so springy I could slide off at any second.

'Thanks.'

I feel paralysed by shyness, even though Amelia was right. I haven't been able to keep my hands far away from Nia all night. But now I'm in the same room with her, alone, with a bed and no one to bother us, I feel unable to talk, let alone touch her.

'I'm not sleepy, though,' she says belatedly.

I chance a look at her. She doesn't look too relaxed either. I wonder if she's been in this situation before. I don't mean in an apartment building with a comatose teenager and a budding wildcrafter, but on a bed with a boy. I'll kid myself she hasn't.

'Me either,' I say. I move next to her and arrange a pillow against the headboard. I haven't bothered to take my boots off. I unbuckle my watch and put it next to the bed.

'It's only ten-thirty in City time.'

'I'd normally still be up, reading.' Nia reaches out and takes my hand, laces her fingers through mine. Looks at me through those lashes. I remind myself to keep breathing. Everything about this situation seems brand new, as if I've never been with a girl before.

'Let's talk for a while, and then if we get bored we can go exploring. Amelia said we can go anywhere on this floor.'

'She only meant you. I don't think she likes me very much.'

'That's just her way. I don't think she cares whether people like her or not.'

'Maybe,' I say, not wanting to disagree with her.

Nia strokes the back of my hand and it nearly drives me wild. I close my eyes for a second.

'Do you think she knows what she's doing?' she asks.

'Not sure.' I've been trying not to think about it too much. If Lupe trusts Amelia, though, that's got to count for something. 'It's worth a try.'

'Why does it have to be you, though?' Nia slides closer to me. She smells sweet, like pears. It must be her shampoo.

'Who else would do it? Paul's my oldest friend. I have to do this.'

I sound less conflicted than I feel.

'So, do you have a game plan?' she asks.

'What do you mean?'

'Amelia said that Paul needed to be coaxed out of the dream. If someone, I mean if *you* need to talk him into doing something he might not want to do…You should think about the best way to get through to him. And you should tell me. We could practise what to say.'

I get a sudden urge to tell her what Doctor Gregory said about Paul. But I don't feel like telling her what happened after, at the velo. Too much. I'll scare her away, right when she's never been closer.

Nia smiles for no reason.

'What is it?' I ask.

'Turn around and look in the mirror.'

I twist my head slowly, reluctant to look away when her face is this close to mine. I see me in the foreground, with Nia's face over my shoulder. Red wallpaper for a backdrop. Marble and velvet and gold. We're from another place and time.

'This mirror sucks,' I say. 'I'm going to wake up and think there's someone else in the room with us. It's gonna give me nightmares.'

'We look good together,' she says. 'I've been thinking…'

'Yeah?' I turn to face her once more.

She opens her mouth to speak but then her whole face scrunches. She covers her face with her hands and sneezes. When it has passed she takes her hands away.

'Take two. I don't want to jinx it by talking about it, Wolfie, but I've decided that we're going out. You and me.'

This is such a surprise I don't say anything at all, but I do reach up and brush a strand of hair off her face.

'If that's okay with you,' she adds. There's a touch of uncertainty in her voice. I lean forward and kiss the tip of her nose in lieu of telling her how amazed I am that she always finds the courage to say these things.

'Yes,' I say. I've pulled off the impossible.

'Good.' The smallest of smiles curves her lips. And then she breathes out, relieved. 'Good. Hand me those pyjamas. I'm cold. I want to get under the covers.'

She begins to do that clever thing girls do when they change shirts and yank their bras out of an armhole without you seeing any flesh. When she's done she flips back the doona and climbs inside.

'You getting in?'

I don't wait to be asked twice. I unlace my boots and join her. Put Delilah's book next to the bed. It's getting dog-eared from being carried in my pocket. Nia wriggles out of her tights under the sheets, flinging them around her head theatrically and across the room. They land in a black puddle on the rose-patterned carpet.

We lie apart, her on her side of the bed, and me on mine. She doesn't bother with the pyjama pants. Her arms are caramel-brown against the white sheets. The sight of her hair spilling over the pillow must be a dream, a dream I think I've had before. She presses on my bruised cheek.

'Did you really go to boxing training or were you in a fight?'

'Boxing training is fighting.'

Nia makes a face. 'No, it's not. I've seen *Rocky*. Boxing training is skipping and punching that bag-thing. Even when you do get biffed, you're wearing an entire mattress strapped to your head, so you don't get hurt.'

'I'm not making it up.' Not really. I roll over and sigh. 'I haven't told you about my day yet. I was going to.'

'Okay.'

Her voice is anxious enough for me to turn my head to look at her.

'I saw Doctor Gregory.'

'On your own?'

I nod. 'He put a letter through my door this morning and I arranged to meet him. I knew he was baiting me, but I thought it was the quickest way to find out more.'

'What happened?'

'Do you remember Sanjay from the club saying Paul was the teacher's pet?'

'He said Paul paid for his dreams differently.'

'According to Doctor Gregory, Paul got the pills in exchange for giving him information about me.'

'No…What sort of information?' Nia's eyes are wide.

'Beats me. He didn't say. But he got to enjoy telling me my best friend has been stabbing me in the back for god knows how long, and I knew nothing about it.'

Nia puts her arm over my shoulder. She thinks for a minute. 'I want to say that Doctor Gregory must be lying, but when I talked to Paul that night, when I deleted the photo, he was guilty about something. Something was eating him up inside, and it wasn't all about Ingrid.'

I move closer to her and bury my face into her neck. Only once I'm close do I worry about how I smell after the amount I've sweated today. It's too late, so I try to put it out of mind.

Nia's bare leg bumps against mine. 'Are you okay?' she asks.

'I don't know.' I lean half-out of the bed to retrieve the book. 'I've been reading more of this book. I didn't find anything more about Night Sickness, but I did find something even more interesting.'

Nia snuggles in to look at the book with me. When I turn the cover over and see the *W&S* stamp again, I realise for the first time that Blake gets her books from Amelia. *WOOKEY & SALAMON*. Man, I'm slow.

'Look at this photograph.'

'Where's the cathedral?' asks Nia. 'I've never seen it.'

'There isn't one, that's the thing. But read this bit.' I

point to the paragraph about the cathedral and the last period of Eternal Night.

'*"Daylight returned in March the following year, ending what had been the Third Night,"*' Nia reads. 'That is so cool. This has all happened before. Why don't you look happy?'

'It's—I don't know. It's weird to think about the Darkness happening here before.'

'But it's going to end—isn't that good news?'

'I'm used to it, though. I'll have to get used to another change.'

'Everything is always changing.' Nia runs her toes up and down my calf. 'Why are you frowning again, Wolfie? You know what you need?'

'What?'

She doesn't tell me but she moves closer.

'What?' I say again.

Nia puts her hand up to my mouth. 'Shut up and come here. There's nothing more to say.'

26

I wake when the world starts heaving as if it's going to crack apart. It takes me a few seconds to realise that I've fallen asleep with my head on Wolfboy's chest, and now he's thrashing wildly.

I fall away and watch from a safer distance. A deep frown scores his face; he looks as if he's bearing the weight of famine and war and every possible natural disaster in his sleep. I've never seen anyone have a nightmare before and it's a scary sight.

'Hey,' I say softly, shaking him. 'Hey, wake up.'

He starts talking then, incoherent mumbles. I wonder if it's the right thing to wake him in the middle of a bad dream. His arms are no longer flying about, so I move in close again, and put my mouth to his ear.

'Wolfie,' I whisper, 'It's me, Nia, wake up.'

His eyes flick open, and he grabs my wrist, gasping. I run my hands up and down his arms, trying to soothe him. I feel as if I'm anchoring him with my touch. Gradually his eyes stop blinking Morse code.

'What were you dreaming about?' The air has got cold in here while we've slept, and my breath forms white clouds.

Wolfboy struggles to talk. 'Ortie and I were waiting at the shop for Diana. She was late and we were worried. When she showed up we were really relieved.'

He still doesn't seem a hundred per cent awake, even though his eyes are open and he's talking.

'But then we realised that there was something wrong with her face. It had been erased. Like someone had taken an eraser and rubbed out her whole face.'

'That sounds horrible,' I say, brushing his hair off his forehead. I wish I knew a comforting bedtime story I could tell him. I make do with whatever comes into my head.

'Ever since I was little I've been able to remember my dreams. I used to drive my mum crazy telling her about them. When I was twelve I had a dream journal, and this dream book where you could look up symbols and what they meant. I don't do that anymore, but sometimes, even now, I'll wake up from a really great dream and get so annoyed that I won't find out what happened. But if I try really hard, sometimes when I fall asleep again I can pick the dream up again, right from where it stopped the last time, like pausing and playing a DVD. It's pretty cool.'

We breathe in time, my head rising and falling on Wolfboy's chest. The room is dark with no windows. It could be any time of day or night.

Wolfboy's eyes melt closed again.

It's so strange and adult to be lying in bed with him, but it's made easier by the fact that he looks like a little boy when he's sleeping. Numbness spreads across my buried left arm but I don't want to move it in case it wakes him.

When I can't bear it any longer, I carefully slide away, my dead arm prickling unbearably as the blood flows back. My phone tells me it's Friday morning. We slept through the night together. Right about now I should be in form room getting my name marked off. I don't even know the school policy on non-attendance, if they'll message Mum or call her.

The hallway is silent and empty, which is just as well, because I'm only wearing a t-shirt and undies. I can't find the switch so I leave the bathroom door ajar, giving me enough light to see.

I use the toilet and wash my hands. In the mirror above the hand basin, I look different. My eyes are bigger, darker, more serious than I'm used to. I touch the cold glass to check it's really me. There's no going back from this now.

When I go back to the guest room I pull on Amelia's pyjama pants and walk through the hushed house. There's a fur-lined jacket hanging on a hook near the stairs, and a pair of gardening clogs. I slip both on, and go up to the roof.

The ladder doesn't seem as daunting this time, but a breeze has sprung up in the last few hours. I walk across the rooftop garden, breathing in the sharp air. My allergies have subsided. The fresh chill is welcome after the red embrace of the guest room, the closeness of everything, Wolfboy's unfamiliar body heat.

I wonder if Wolfboy and I have done something wrong, getting together while Paul sleeps on downstairs, lost and alone.

I go to the edge of the roof. The fake forest looks smaller from up here, but I can see now that there's a pattern to the trees. At the centre is a circular bald patch.

Beyond the fake forest pokes the black outline of Orphanville, a handful of fingers on the horizon. It's difficult to imagine Orphanville minus the Kidds. I look to the left, trying to see the snaking river that divides the city, but I'm not high enough. I think of Mum with her sister and my cousins in Fish Creek, and even though I chose not to go, I feel left out.

When I look back there's an odd rainbow light building in the heart of the fake forest. At first I think I'm imagining it, but it becomes obvious that the glow is strengthening. As it gets brighter, the light separates into distinct pinpricks, a galaxy of different colours scattered through the plywood trees. I thought the forest was eerie earlier, but the lights turn it into something resembling fairyland. I have to see it close up.

The forest is beautiful, painted in mingling multi-coloured lights that lift the worst of the shadows. The ground under my feet sharpens into splinters of shaved wood; the trees have clear zigzag edges. The forest is as silent as ever.

I stop at the foot of a tree and look up high. Tiny LED lights are built into the wood, maybe twenty or thirty on each tree. I run my eyes down to the base, where it's hammered into the ground, but I can't see any wiring. How is it done?

I keep walking. After a minute or so the trees thin out; I'm getting close to the centre. A low buzzing sound gets louder as the trees get thinner. I don't feel scared, at least I don't think I do, but my feet start to drag. What is that sound?

As I get closer to the source the noise becomes more familiar.

Whirring.

Then a laugh, a child's laugh, and the bass murmur of an adult's voice in response.

I creep closer, using the trees to mask my progress. Through the cutout shapes I see two people. I reach the last tree before the clearing and I hide behind it.

At the centre of the forest is something far more strange than the galaxy of rainbow lights. A little girl is riding an exercise bike with an enthusiastic grin. The bike is set into concrete in the middle of the sawdust clearing. Even though the seat on the bike is on the lowest setting, the girl's feet barely reach the pedals. As I watch she slips off the seat and rides standing. She is laughing and puffing.

Her dad stands behind her, close enough to catch her if she falls. The little girl is about five years old and as cute as they come in mismatched red and pink clothes and a pudding bowl haircut. She's getting tired, and as her feet slow I see she's wearing gumboots with rainbows on them. The twinkling lights dim and flicker.

'Can I have a go?' asks her dad. 'You're hogging it. Let me have a go.' He's dressed formally, in a suit, and I wonder what on earth they're doing in the forest at this early hour. But I guess when it's always night, playtime could be any time.

The little girl shakes her head and steps up her pedalling again. The lights get brighter. Her dad backs away, resigned to not getting a turn. A red birthmark over his eye is just visible through the lens of his black-rimmed glasses. I'm lucky he's busy watching his daughter, and not looking in my direction. He can't take his eyes off her.

A tear, uninvited and unexpected, slides down my cheek. I blink it away and that's it. I don't even feel sad. The girl lifts her head and looks dangerously close to where I'm hiding. I move away before I'm seen.

twenty-seven

I'm alone when I wake. There's only a Nia-shaped absence in the bed. I roll over to the empty space and breathe in the sugary smell left on the pillow. My body is leaden, usually a sign that I've spent the night fighting dark dreams. I hope I didn't sleep-talk.

I want her to spend another night with me, and then another. I don't want this to be the first and only time. Whispery dream remnants still hang about, but I can't grab on to them. Someone's blank oval face, oceans of fear. Was I dreaming about Paul?

When I think I can move, I pick up my phone from the bedside table. Nia's is next to mine, so she can't have gone far.

I dial and I can tell the phone is ringing in an empty house. Echoing up the stairs from the Birds In Winter shop. I hang up. I've slept through the morning, and now that it's afternoon they're probably at the park or shopping. I'll try again later.

I find yesterday's clothes crumpled on the floor, then follow the sound of muffled voices to Amelia's main room. Blake, Amelia and Nia sit on the floor with a teapot, cups and plates of food. All three look up as I enter the room, and I blush under their collective gaze. I don't know enough about the ways of girls to tell if Nia has talked about what we did last night.

The girls have moved Paul to a chaise longue at the side of the room. I go to him first. He looks the same as yesterday, only perhaps more waxen. I always thought Paul, more than any of us, had stayed the same since the Darkness. But it turns out he was changing right under my eyes and I didn't notice. I know how lonely that feels.

'Nothing happened overnight,' says Blake. 'All his vitals are the same.' She holds up her notebook. 'I recorded them here. Every hour.' She keeps her voice clinical but I can see her worry has grown. She's not alone.

'He isn't twitching as much anymore,' I say.

'That means he's gone in deeper,' says Amelia. 'We need to move faster. I'm waiting for something to distil, but as soon as it's done, we're good to go. We're supposed to wait until the moon is at its apex, but I think we should do it as soon as we can.'

I leave Paul and sit next to Nia. She moves her teacup out of the way and smiles at me. Our eyes click. I feel something shift deep down in my stomach. Her t-shirt has slipped, exposing a patch of round brown shoulder. All the natural laws pull me towards her. I have to force myself to stay where I am. There are other people in the room now.

'Doughnut?' she asks, holding a plate in front of me. I notice she's getting dark circles under her eyes, like a Local. 'Blake made them.'

The doughnuts are golf-ball sized and dusted with cinnamon and sugar. They're warm and delicious.

'Take another. There's no way you can eat just one.'

After I've grabbed three more, I put the plate down. Nia rests her hand on my knee.

'Did you stay up all night?' I ask Blake.

'Sort of. I slept inbetween checking on Paul.'

'You need to get some more sleep.'

'I'm fine,' she says, but her words are undermined by a yawn so large it shakes her entire body.

'He's right,' says Amelia. She wears a thick leather apron and her hands are stained purple. 'You should sleep. I have more prep to do, but I can manage it on my own.'

'We'll stay in here and watch Paul.' I help myself to

more doughnuts, then offer the plate to Nia, but she waves them away.

'Had too many already?'

She shakes her head, an inscrutable expression on her face. 'Not eating.'

'Why?' Next to me Blake freezes in the middle of pouring a cup of tea. Nia still doesn't answer. I take another bite. 'Why?'

'Don't be angry,' she says.

Blake titters nervously. Amelia turns to me. 'It's best to fast before taking the dream meds. It works quicker, and it's more effective.'

I still have a mouth full of half-chewed doughnut. Only manners stop me from spitting it out. 'What? Then why did everyone let me eat five doughnuts in a row?'

'Because I'm going to do the dream.' Nia looks scared and so she should.

'You tricked me.' The doughnut sticks in my throat when I try to swallow it.

'Hear me out, I've got really good reasons, just let me—'

I cut her off and turn to Amelia. 'How long do you have to fast? There's still time, right?'

'Overnight is best.'

I stare at her.

'There's not really time.' She smiles wryly.

Blake stands up, holding the teapot and a stack of cups.

She hurries out of the room. I expect Amelia to exit as well, but she leans back and watches. I realise she doesn't trust me. She doesn't want to leave Nia on her own with me right now, while I'm so pissed off. I force myself to unclench my hands.

'Wolfie, I spent the entire night watching you thrashing about having bad dreams.' Nia tries to put her hand on my arm, but I shrug her off. It doesn't stop her from talking, though. 'I can do this. I never have nightmares, and I told you about how I can direct my own dreams. That's a skill. Not everyone can do that.'

'Remember what I said about lucid dreaming,' Amelia butts in. I shoot her a pissed-off glare, which she returns calmly. I get the feeling she wouldn't think twice about chucking me out of her home if I misbehaved. Nia's torrent of words continues.

'Not only am I better suited to take the dream, I'm kind of responsible, in a roundabout sort of way. If I hadn't deleted Ingrid's photo, then maybe Paul wouldn't have gone off the deep end.'

I open my mouth to argue, but she holds her finger up.

'If you say I can't do this—and actually, I'd like to see you find a way to stop me—you're denying me the opportunity to set things right. Do you want me to be wracked with guilt for the rest of my days? You could be karmically cursing me for several lifetimes.'

I look from Amelia to Nia and down to the almost-demolished plate of doughnuts.

'It's done anyway, it's too late now,' Nia says.

I look at her, with her wide eyes and her bed-mussed hair, and I feel so tired I can't believe I just got out of bed.

28

The rooftop is bathed in full-moon silver. It looks like a sports pitch lit for a night match. Amelia looks up at the moon, clinical and round and white, not quite directly overhead.

'We need to move quickly now,' she says.

Blake draws a large circle on the concrete with white chalk. I shiver when the wind manages to burrow inside the overalls I borrowed off Amelia. I no longer feel like a tough lady mechanic. I try to catch Wolfboy's eye for comfort, but he's over at the edge of the roof, still concentrating on being pissed off and brooding.

'Wildgirl, take off your shoes and make yourself comfortable in there.'

Amelia drops to her knees at the edge of the circle.

I ponder the impossibility of feeling comfortable under these circumstances. I settle for kicking off my shoes and letting my hair out of its ponytail. While Amelia has been talking Blake has set up another pillow next to Paul. I try not to look at it. Amelia has a silver tea tray before her, crowded with jars and bottles and cups and a genuine Wedgwood teapot.

My heartbeat starts off on a leisurely tour of my body, pulsing along my temples, throat, fingers. It settles finally in my hollow stomach.

Wolfboy finally quits his sulking. He comes over and wraps me in his arms, holding me too tight.

'Don't do this,' he mumbles close to my ear, but there's no conviction in his voice. He knows this is a done deal.

'I'm going to be fine.'

These are just words, of course. I do know there's no way Wolfboy should do this in my place. If we had to break into the Datura Institute, fight off some black-belt sleep nurses, hog-tie Doctor Gregory and abseil off the roof, then I would be happy to let him take care of it. Someone has to go in after Paul and I'm the best candidate. We each have to play to our strengths.

'I knew you wouldn't back out, so I've been thinking about what you can do,' he says. 'I think Paul is stuck in the past or something. I don't know if that helps.'

'Okay.'

'Be careful, Wildgirl.'

I look at his oceanic eyes and his too-serious, too-beautiful face. I think of last night and all the things we did, and I feel unaccountably embarrassed and pleased, all at the same time. I kiss him. Then I step across the line, dodging the four large crystals placed along the perimeter.

Amelia pours from the teapot into a glass, then uses a pipette to add extra ingredients. She waves Blake away from the circle.

Amelia hands me the blue pill that we got from Umbra, and a bottle of water. I neck the pill, automatically running through every warning my mum ever gave me about taking drugs. Wolfboy and Blake settle in to spectate at the edge of the circle.

'You need to wear this.' Amelia holds up a chunky silver necklace studded with gemstones. I can't help scrunching up my face. It's one fugly piece of bling.

'Amethyst and moonstone,' Amelia says in response to my disgust. 'They'll protect you from nightmares and keep the dream clear from influence.'

'This is a bit woo-woo for me.'

'Wildgirl, you're about to enter someone else's dreams. That's about as woo-woo as it gets.'

Amelia stands behind me and fastens the clasp. She puts her mouth close to my ear and whispers just loudly enough for me to hear. 'I've never seen anyone go under for this long, but I read through my grandfather's notes again. It's rare for someone to wake up past the twenty-four hour point. You need to do this as quickly as you can.'

The metal links of the necklace are cold and heavy. I look across the flimsy border of the chalk line at Wolfboy. I know Amelia's words should bother me, but the whole thing is starting to feel pleasingly cinematic. 'What do I do now?'

'Let's sit down and have a chat.' Amelia speaks loudly, more for Wolfboy and Blake's benefit than mine.

We sit on the rug, facing each other. I'm as clear and crisp as a swimming pool full of fizzy mineral water. I wonder how long the pill will take to work. I picture it buzzing in my bloodstream and making its way to my brain.

'In a few minutes I'll give you my medicine to drink. You should find yourself feeling sleepy soon after. When you're dreaming it's important that you don't impose your will too strongly. You have to find Paul's dream first, rather than making him come into yours.' She mouths the final word soundlessly: 'Fast.'

'Okay.' I look at Amelia, taking in her features. In this light it's clear she's chosen the right colour scheme for herself. Midnight hair, blue eyes, red lips. Under normal circumstances I would probably find her tone bossy, but I'm enjoying listening to her talk like a queen.

'Amelia? What's the circle for?' The words take a while to bubble out of my mouth.

'It binds you and Paul together, stops you from being interested in anyone else's thoughts.'

The thought of me being interested in anything outside the circle is laughable. It's the most perfect and complete circle I've ever seen. The chalk line burns whitely into the grey concrete. Amelia hands me a mug. It has a chipped rim and a teddy bear on the side. I want to tell Amelia how funny this is, the chip and the bear, so ordinary, especially compared to the fancy teapot, but I can't be bothered opening my mouth. The medicine is river-water brown.

'There's no need to drink it all. Swallow two mouthfuls.'

The liquid hits my lips and it tastes foul, but I force myself to take a gulp. Bitter, but not as thick as it looks.

'Easy, tiger. Enough.'

Amelia takes the mug from me and crawls outside the circle. 'Lie back,' she says.

I find the pillow and let my head fall against it. The ground is hard underneath me; the stars are billion-carat diamonds above.

I close my eyes.

I think I'm a better person when I'm in Shyness. Stronger. Braver. I try to breathe slowly, willing my body to slow down, relax. But it doesn't work. Even though my body feels like melted cheese, my rebellious mind is still razor-sharp. I forgot to ask Amelia how to exit the dream quickly, in case there's an emergency. I forgot to ask her how we wake up, once I've talked some sense into Paul.

'One more question,' I say, and open my eyes, expecting to see the night above me. But the sky isn't there anymore.

I lie very still and ponder the roof above me. Water-stained with a ceiling rose at the centre.

'It's not working,' I say again.

I twitch my fingers experimentally, feeling the cool touch of leather underneath them. I lift my head, push up on my elbows. It takes a full thirty seconds to realise where I am.

I'm in Paul and Thom's cottage, the historical house in the middle of the Memorial Gardens. Wolfboy and I visited it after escaping Orphanville on the night we met. I recognise the cracked leather couches, and the austere furniture. Sideboard, writing desk, Tiffany lamp. Around the corner there's a handbasin, for sure.

I roll off the couch to check. There it is. For some reason the sight of the apple-green basin makes me smile. The cottage. What a strange place to teleport to. There are hooks on the wall, with bath towels hanging on them. I don't remember those being there last time, although maybe I just didn't notice.

There are other differences in the cottage. A throw rug on the couch. A futon in the corner. A bar fridge. An Andy Warhol Marilyn poster on the wall. Fewer dirty clothes lying about, less crap in general. Something is not quite right.

When I figure it out, I feel incredibly stupid.

This is the dream.

I slap my palm to my head. What a dufus. How could I forget I was supposed to dream? It feels so real. I run my hands over Amelia's overalls. You'd think my subconscious could have arranged a ballgown or something. The amethyst and moonstone necklace still rests heavily on my collarbone, but my feet feel different. I have heavy leather boots on. I march my feet up and down and the floor feels one hundred per cent real.

What else can I try?

I grab a nearby glass and fill it at the basin. The water is cold and slick and real as it travels down my throat. When I put the glass back down on the sideboard it makes a sound like hands slapping together.

I lift the glass up and place it down again.

Clap!

The clapping continues, even though I leave the glass where it is. Slow clapping at first, then flamenco-fast. The sound echoes through the empty cottage. I can't tell where it's coming from. I turn in circles. The sound gets louder, until it's more like the explosion of distant grenades.

I remember that there's supposed to be someone else in this dream, not just me. Someone I'm supposed to look for. I touch the necklace and I hear a voice in my head: 'FAST.'

I rush to the front door and fling it open. There are no gardens outside the cottage, no path that leads to the avenue of fallen trees. Instead there's another room, an unfamiliar one this time. The room is at least thirty metres long, with orange walls and white opaque panels lit from behind. Two rows of reclining day beds along the side walls, with a carpeted path down the centre leading to another set of double doors.

Everything smooth and modular. A space-station day spa. Some of the thickly padded seats are occupied.

I half-run down the aisle, stopping at the foot of a bed. A man lies on it asleep, a pair of headphones clamped over his ears. He looks peaceful. A neatly dressed woman watches over him, clipboard in hand. She doesn't notice me. I squint at her name-badge. Two flowers. Annie. The Datura Institute.

I move on. I'm drawn to the end of the room, the bed closest to the next set of doors. This bed is occupied by someone dressed for combat in camouflage pants and a shirt.

He's asleep, still, arms falling on either side of the padded chair. I squeeze into the space between the chairs to get a look at his face, accidentally knocking a video game controller off the bedside table. 'Paul. Come with me now,' I say.

Paul's eyes snap open as if he's been shot with adrenaline. He draws a sharp breath. Off the bed, on his feet, and out the doors.

He's gone before I even have time to register what's happened. Compared to him I move in slow motion. I push on the heavy door, slip through into darkness, a yawning night landscape.

A newly mown soccer field with crisp white lines intersecting the green grass. An enormous hemisphere of sky, with the eyeball moon riding high. When I look behind me there's no doorway, no cottage, no building, no sign of Paul. A thick forest extends as far as I can see.

I have something clutched in my hands. It's a machine gun.

'Incoming!' someone screeches and bolts past me.

A booming explosion sends me running after him. It's hard to move with the heavy gun; I need both hands to hold it, and it bangs against my thighs. The soldier beckons me onwards and I recognise Paul's face under his helmet. His scrawny frame has been made bulky by bullet belts and drink canteens and mini-satchels slung over him.

The final piece slips into place. I'm in Paul's dream. I've actually done it.

29

'Paul! Paul, wait up.'

I lope awkwardly, comforted only by the fact that Paul must be struggling more than I am, given his load. There's another cataclysmic boom behind me. I expect to see fire lighting up the forest, and dust and shrapnel, but there's nothing.

'Seriously—Paul!'

I stumble on the grass. All I have to do is look at a sports field and I completely lose all sense of coordination. I can't let him get away.

Paul ignores me, hefting his gun onto his shoulder and bellowing like his cargo pants are on fire. Beyond the soccer field there's a path running alongside a creek.

The creek looks familiar; it could be the creek that leads to Orphanville.

I discover that this stupid commando dream is real enough that I'm gasping for breath. All I have to do is catch him, talk him into returning to his waking life pronto, and then we're done here. This needs to be over in five minutes.

Paul swings his gun from side to side as he runs. It's so weird to see him galloping about when I know he's actually lying on Amelia's roof, deathly still. Ahead, the creek peels off to the right, while the path tunnels through a hill.

'Bam,' he yells. 'Bam bam.'

At least one thing is certain: I have no control over this dream. Amelia's worry that I would exert too much influence is completely unfounded. Paul has already run headlong into the circular black mouth of the tunnel.

My legs slow without consulting my brain. The tunnel looks less like an innocent method of getting from point A to point B, and more like a dark vortex that wants to suck every bit of hope from me.

But I do not want to get lost in Paul's dream, and I do not want to lose him. I walk into the tunnel, my footsteps instantly louder, telling myself it's not real.

I sense damp concrete around me. There's nothing visible behind me, just darkness. Ahead of me there's more nothingness. I should be able to hear Paul's footsteps in front of me, but I can't. The thought that I am also lying deathly still on Amelia's rooftop grabs me by the throat.

The dark is so complete I lose sense of where my body is in space. My mum's face comes to me, then my dead nan's. The tunnel might be Paul's but I'm pretty sure my thoughts are still my thoughts.

'Mum?'

My voice is high and uncertain. I don't expect a reply.

'Nia. Nia, there you are.' Mum's disembodied voice sounds relieved. 'He's trapped me. I don't think I'm going to get out of here alive. I want you to promise—'

'Where are you? Mum?'

The panic I've been trying to keep down rises up. I've been a bitch to my mum. I need to cut her some slack. I look frantically for an exit when I'm suddenly doused in burning white light. I hold my hands to my face.

There's a roar, a crowd cheering. If Mum says anything else she's drowned out.

When my eyes clear I am no longer in a tunnel but on a stage with lights and a gawking crowd outside, beyond a wire fence. Paul stands nearby, in normal clothes, talking to a girl. I look up to see that the wire fence extends overhead and around us, a cube.

When I look down I'm wearing a shiny black catsuit. It clings from my neck all the way down to my ankles. I'd never, ever in my life choose to wear something this tight.

The back of it pulls strangely. I crane my head and see a long tail trailing behind me.

'For fuck's sake,' I say. I close my eyes and try to enact some *I Dream of Jeannie*-style magic on my outfit. When I open my eyes, though, nothing has changed. The fact that every person here is imaginary does little to comfort me.

'You really gotta work out your objectification of women, Paul,' I call out. 'A cage? Really?'

Paul turns on me with annoyance. 'Shut up. You're not even supposed to be here.'

He turns back to the girl, who smiles at him. It's Ingrid. She's wearing the same jacket and denim mini skirt as in the deleted photo.

As I watch, Paul and Ingrid engage in a strange ritual. First Paul brings his head down to hers, butting her gently on the forehead.

'Ouch,' says Ingrid, even though it couldn't have hurt at all. Then she leans forward and bops her head into his.

'Ouch,' Paul says, and then they kiss. This is obviously what the crowd is here to see because there's a collective sigh and a surge of interest behind me. An audience member pokes me through the mesh. I start to tell them to quit it, when I see it's the little girl from the forest, the one who was pedal-powering the lights.

'Jethro,' she says.

'Hi,' I say, then turn back. I can't think about Wolfboy.

I have more important things to worry about. If Paul is hooking up with his ex in his dream, then no wonder he doesn't want to come out of it. How can I convince him to leave her behind?

'Hey, hey, guys.' Paul and Ingrid break apart. 'Hey Ingrid, did you notice the obscene outfit Paul chose for me? How do you feel about this cage? Make you feel good?'

Paul practically shoots laser-beams of rage out of his eyes. 'Shut. Up.' He grabs Ingrid's arm urgently. 'Say it. Like we practised.'

'I made a mistake when I broke up with you,' declares Ingrid. 'I was scared of the terrible power of my love. I miss you every day, I think about you every hour.'

Her eyes roam distractedly. She isn't saying her soap opera lines with any conviction. Maybe I won't have to convince him. Maybe Ingrid will do it for me. The crowd begins to boo. Paul tries to hush them, but the hubbub grows.

Ingrid hangs her head, defeated. 'I can't do this anymore, Paul.'

'Why are you being like this?' Paul's voice is high and hurt and oh so young. 'If you want me to hang out with your friends more, I can. I can be different. You have to give me another chance.'

'No.' Ingrid shakes her head.

'Who do you want me to be? I can be that guy!'

Ingrid looks at him sadly, and then flickers. Her body wavers at the edges; she blurs, sharpens, blurs again. With a 'zip' she vanishes inwards, pulled into a central dot that disappears. A TV being switched off. Gone.

Paul spins around, shocked, looking for her in the cage. Instead he sees me.

'Oh no,' I say, holding up my hands.

He points an accusatory finger. 'This isn't how it goes. It's you again. You made it turn out wrong.'

I don't wait for him to leap. I turn and run, prepared to claw my way out of the cage if necessary. But the cage isn't there anymore, and neither are the crowds. We're in a dusty lifeless plain.

I pound across the sandy ground, with no idea where I'm headed. Paul's feet thump behind mine. I can't let him catch me. My stupid tail threatens to tangle around my ankles and the heavy necklace bounces into my face.

The horizon breaks ahead. There's a precipice, a cliff, beyond which there's nothing but air. Paul's so close I can hear his laboured breath matching mine. I prepare to hit the ground, rolling and grazed.

It never happens. Paul shoots past me, picking up speed. All too slowly I figure out what's happening.

'No!' I try to shout, but it's too late. Paul swan-dives off the cliff, hanging in midair before knifing downwards. It would be beautiful if it wasn't so terrible.

I skid to a halt at the edge of the cliff, dust rising around me.

Paul hits the black river rushing below. I have a split second to decide. My decision is to not jump to my death. But everyone is counting on me to rescue Paul. I can't give up on him. And I can't die in a dream, I don't think, even it feels real.

I jump.

I hold my nose and free-fall, feet first. My body pierces the black water. Icy. I plunge downwards for what seems a long time. My feet touch the bottom and I push up. I'm wearing the overalls again, and that's a pity because they are twisted and heavy with water, dragging me down.

I suck in air when I surface. The water is so cold it crushes my chest. Already the current is carrying me downstream. I see Paul, twenty metres ahead, clinging to a rock. I thrash out some freestyle until I reach him.

'Paul!' I say. 'Paul, listen to me!'

His eyes are closed, his mouth opening at all the wrong times, making him take in mouthfuls of water.

'Paul, that wasn't me or Ingrid making that happen back there. That was you, your mind. You know it's over, you know it's time to let her go.'

'No,' he says, opening one eye. 'No way.'

His fingers slip and he throws his arm over the rock with gargantuan effort.

'Let go of the fucking rock, Paul!' I bash his fingers, then latch on to him before he floats away.

'Don't struggle. I'm trying to help you.'

Paul elbows me in the head.

As my head snaps back, I catch a glimpse of the strangest thing: the rainbow-booted girl from the forest again, above us, torpedoing through the star-speckled sky like Astro Boy. A wavelet dumps on my face, blinding me. I blink away the water but she's gone.

A surge of water lifts me high, and then I hit solid land, hard.

'Ow!'

It's no longer full night. I push my hair out of my face. There's river grit in my mouth.

I sit up and spit on the ground.

This has to be a joke. I'm lying on a bed of moss. The river is clear and burbling. Behind me is a waving meadow. The sky is pastel-streaky. I've been beached in the most gorgeous fantasy place Paul could imagine. Pretty soon some dancing squirrels are going to sing a jaunty song about gathering acorns.

Paul lies several metres away on the mossy beach. He's drenched, like me, but seems unhurt.

'Where are we?' he asks.

'I've got no idea.'

Paul cranes to look behind us at the meadow.

'The sun is rising,' he says. It's true. Paul's face takes on a warm tint as the sun begins its ascent.

It's a fully formed circle before either of us will admit there's something wrong.

'Oh no,' says Paul.

The sun is rising, sure, but it's a black sun in an orange sky. It rises faster than it should; a black circle luminous with dark fire.

'No, no, no.' Paul tosses his head from side to side. 'I'm not ready to wake up.' Tears gather and fall; I can't tell if they're tears of defeat or fear.

'Paul.' I crawl across to him, holding on to his hand. 'You're ready. Trust me.'

He won't look at me, but it doesn't matter because the ground starts to disintegrate beneath us, the moss melts away, and we're falling down towards the centre of the earth.

thirty

The twitching stops, and both Wildgirl and Paul lie still. Too still. The sudden peace bothers me. 'It's gone on too long,' I say to Amelia. 'I think we should wake them.'

'Don't even think about stepping over that line, Wolfboy.'

I look down. I had no idea my feet had taken me to the edge of the circle. Blake sits on the periphery, looking cold and miserable. I pull Amelia away.

'You admitted that you've never done this before.' It's difficult to keep my voice low. I think of Delilah's book, the hidden histories of Shyness, and wonder how much Amelia might know that I don't.

Amelia is stubborn. 'I've read accounts written in my own grandfather's hand, and I followed the instructions to a T.'

'The medicine could work differently with Nia, or—'

Nia gasps loudly, as if she's heard me say her name.

'Meels—quick!' Blake leans over the line.

Nia arches and her eyes snap open. After a few seconds her body relaxes and she's instantly soaked to the skin, as if she's been water-bombed from above.

It's too much for Blake, who crawls away so fast she falls over. I jump across the line and kneel at Nia's side. When she sees my face hovering over hers, she smiles radiantly.

'Dark again.'

A wave of euphoria pulses from her. She gulps a few times, as if she's just swum to the surface from the ocean depths. I pull her rag-doll body to a sitting position. Her overalls are plastered to her body. Strands of wet hair latch onto me.

'So trippy, Wolfie. Amazing.'

'You're back,' I say inadequately. 'Did it work? Are you okay? Are you hurt?'

'Wolfie, I'm fine.' Nia swallows. 'It worked. Go to Paul.'

Paul has woken too, though far less dramatically. He lies on his side without making a sound. His face is a river of tears. I look at Nia, and I'm torn.

'Go to him,' she says again, and I obey.

Paul is also sopping wet, his long-sleeved t-shirt clinging to his scrawny chest.

'Buddy,' I say, touching his shoulder. 'It's Jethro. You're safe.'

He blinks. I also offer him help to sit up, but I don't hug him.

'Hurts,' he says through chattering teeth.

'Where?'

'Everywhere.' He puts his fist to his chest and wheezes. Something in that gesture reminds me of the weeks after Gram passed away, and the pain I felt deep in my chest, real physical pain in my body.

'I know.'

'My whole body hurts,' he says, 'I think I'm going to die.'

I rub his back, trying to warm him. 'Paul, you're not going to die. Do you remember what happened?'

His brow furrows. 'Hellcats and Rambo, and...'

'No, I mean you've been asleep. For a while.'

'Yeah?' Paul looks sceptical, and then he remembers something that makes him wince. 'Oh, fuck.'

'Wolfboy,' Amelia calls out. 'Let's get them inside. Hot showers all round.'

I let Paul lean into my side, and Blake and Amelia cross their arms to make a seat for Nia.

'For god's sake, I can walk. I'm not an invalid,' she says, just as her legs buckle underneath her.

Paul and I sprawl on the floor in the drying room, the warmest room in the house. Above our heads hangs an upside-down forest of leaves and branches, tied into bundles and pegged to washing lines.

Paul has stopped shivering. He was so uncharacteristically silent in those first few minutes I wondered if dreaming for too long could damage a person's brain. But the shower seems to have brought him back to life.

'So, you and Wildgirl are together now?'

I was planning on keeping that under wraps for a while, avoid rubbing it in his face, but it must be obvious.

'Yeah. I guess so. I don't know how it's going to work.' I trace patterns over the dusty floor. It smells of eucalyptus and burning wood in here. 'She's still at school, and we live so far apart.'

'Nah, you'll find a way,' he says. 'That's good. I'm happy for you.'

There's more to it than that, but I don't want to bother Paul with my complete range of doubts. Nia might find me interesting now, but after high school it might be different. The more she learns at university, the more she'll realise how little I know.

'She was at our house, right?' Paul asks. 'I mean your

house. She, uh, came into my bedroom and talked to me. That wasn't part of a dream, was it?'

He's having trouble meeting my eyes.

'No, that bit was real,' I say.

'Oh crap.' He hits his leg. 'Crap, crap, crap.'

'Yeah.'

'I can't believe I hit a girl. Why would she help me after I was such a prick to her?'

'Just apologise to her. It's no big deal.'

Paul tucks some stray damp bits of hair behind his ears. 'I did bad things, Jethro. If I tell you, you'll hate me.'

His default expression is still one of abject misery.

'What did you tell Doctor Gregory about me?'

Paul is shocked, freezing with his legs stretched out in front of him. I realise he has no idea how much I've figured out about what's been going on.

'I'm a shit friend. Oh man, I am the shittiest friend.'

He wipes his eyes with the back of his hands, trying to hide what he's doing. The only other time I've seen Paul cry was when he got hit in the teeth with a cricket bat when he was fourteen. And that time Diana made us watch *Bambi*.

'I didn't mean for that to happen. I thought I could go to the institute and stay away from Doctor Gregory. I knew you didn't like him. The last thing I meant to do was go behind your back. I didn't expect I would need it so much.'

'Why did you even go there in the first place? You hate Dreamers.'

'I'd run out of ways to make myself feel better.' Paul sniffles, wipes his nose on the hem of his t-shirt. 'I liked it there. You could relax and read and drink as much coke as you wanted and play video games. The place is totally sci-fi inside. There are these pretty Psych students that work there, come and ask you questions and monitor you.'

It does sound like Paul's idea of heaven. He continues, his voice calmer. 'Remember when you were little and you got sick and your mum would come and read to you in bed and feed you soup and stuff? And you knew you were the most important person in the world?'

I nod.

'Or if you went to a party with your folks and you'd fall asleep on the couch? And when it was time to leave, your dad would carry you out to the car, and then from the car to your bed when you got home. That was the feeling I got at the institute. Like someone was looking after me. I knew it was fake, but I didn't care.'

'It sounds nice,' I say. It's not the nightmare vision of the place I've been forming. I wouldn't have gone near the institute myself, but I understand why Paul did. He's always liked having people around him more than I do. 'I've been talking to some of the people in the program, though, and they say that their dreams get taken. Recorded somehow. Is that true?'

'That's what they tell you. There's a machine that records brainwaves and things, but I don't know if that's what they're really doing.' Paul turns red. 'I haven't answered your question, have I?'

'No.'

'Doctor Gregory singled me out on my second visit, took me into a private consultation room. He said I could help him with his research. The first few sessions were about me, my family, school, what I did in my spare time. Then he started asking about you.'

'What did he ask?'

Paul blows out a thin stream of breath. 'Everything. Nothing. Stupid things. What you were like in kinder and primary school. Did you get along with your parents. Your brother. What you ate for breakfast, were you good at sports, did you ever live near electrical towers, did you like girls. Did you ever play violent computer games, did we ever pretend to be superheroes. Did you grow faster than the other kids. He didn't seem to have a plan at all. He went over the same things, again and again. It didn't seem very scientific.'

I'm silent for a few seconds, mulling this over. There's a rustle near the door. Nia trails her fingers through the canopy of leaves.

'There you are,' she says, crawling over to where we sit, managing to bring a mug with her and not spill what's inside. I put my hand on her leg when she gets to me. She's wearing her school PE outfit. She looks a bit pale, but maybe that's due to lack of sleep.

Nia hands the mug to Paul. 'From Amelia,' she says. 'Some kind of recovery drink. I had mine. I highly recommend it.'

I touch the end of her nose. 'How are you feeling?'

'I feel fantastic, actually. How about you, Paul?'

'Okay, I suppose.' His voice is strangled.

'What have you boys been talking about then? Has Paul told you about the wild dream yet?'

'Nia,' Paul breaks in. 'I just want to tell you how sorry I am, really sorry that I—'

Nia pats him on the back. 'I know, Paul. But thank you for your apology. And seriously, chug that drink.'

'We've been talking about what a creep Doctor Gregory is,' I say, looking at Nia doubtfully. She's having trouble keeping still. Her fingers drum against mine.

'Good, good,' she says. Her eyes are mirror-bright. 'Because I've got to tell you, I woke up in a *vengeful* mood.'

thirty-one

'I think it's, yeah it's—here.' Paul drags the clinking, rustling plastic bag out of the tree hollow. He pulls out a spray can and tests its nozzle on the gravel. 'We've only got black and red, but that will do, right?'

'Perfect.' Nia claps her hands.

'Can't believe you're still caught up in your life of petty crime,' I say.

'Hey,' Paul protests, 'Graffiti is self-expression of the highest form. Let's go before anyone figures out my secret hiding place. I want to keep using this tree.'

His hair is still damp and his clothes borrowed, but he looks like the old Paul returned. Not just pre-dream Paul, but pre-Ingrid Paul. We cross the vacant lot and return to Grey Street.

The Shyness side of the road is a dark ribbon, but the other side glows with the soft burn of late afternoon. I watch a Panwood mum herd her three children into a four-wheel drive, looking fearfully at us like we're going to mug them. I wave at her. She slams the car door and rushes to the driver's side.

Nia skips ahead of us, skips backwards, talking and waving her hands about, conducting the air. She wears every part of her school uniform at once, plus Amelia's winter coat.

'I think I remember where it is. It's this way. Who's going to do it? Should we all do a bit?'

She leaps up and tries to slap a broken shop sign that hangs over the footpath. It pleases her so much, she takes a running stab at the next sign. The Shyness footpaths are riddled with cracks and holes. I hope she doesn't trip and break her leg. At least she gets the left turn onto Saturnalia Avenue right.

I ask Paul. 'Are you feeling as good as she is after that drink?'

Paul swings the bag as he walks. 'I don't think anyone in the world is feeling as good as she is right now.'

'You got that right.'

I'm hoping that at least a small part of her hyper mood

might have something to do with me. With us.

'I still feel bad about what I did,' Paul says.

'You have to stop torturing yourself,' I say, turning when I realise we've already passed the old milk bar. 'We all have to stop torturing ourselves. Nia. Nia, you've gone too far. It's here.'

Doctor Gregory's 'Dream a Little Dream' billboard is still unblemished. I feel less than ever now when I see his big orange head, but this time I notice the tiny datura flowers and a toll-free phone number in the bottom corner of the poster.

'Hey, new poster,' says Nia, looking up. 'Still Doctor Knobhead, but different.'

'Right, you're up,' says Paul, dropping the bag on the ground and handing me a red spray can.

'Me?' I try to hand the can back. 'Why me?'

Nia joins us. 'Because vengeance is yours. Well, vengeance should be yours. If anyone should give Doctor Gregory a big old symbolic bitch-slap, it's you.'

'Also,' says Paul, 'I don't think either Nia or I are going to be able to reach.'

I look down at the can. 'This is stupid.'

Nia grabs the can out of my hand and shakes it, before handing it back. 'Sometimes stupid is all we've got.'

I climb the ladder all the way to the bottom edge of the poster, and then inch along the narrow metal gangway. I begin drawing. The paint sprays in fits and starts at first, but after a few shakes it comes good.

I concentrate on getting the lines right but it's difficult to tell from this close up.

'What is that?' yells Nia. 'What are you drawing?'

'Try and shade it a bit on the right,' Paul says. He understands my vision.

'Oh. Oh.' Nia laughs when she gets it.

When I've finished I climb down. I put my arm across Nia's shoulders as the three of us look at my artwork.

'Beautiful,' pronounces Paul. 'And anatomically correct.'

'That felt surprisingly good,' I say. 'If my parents could see this, they'd be so proud.'

'Do you think?' says Paul, missing my point.

I give him an incredulous look. 'Dude, you know my dad almost as well as I do. He doesn't do proud. At least not where I'm concerned.'

Paul tilts his head. 'Oh. Yeah, I was just thinking. The whole time I was at the institute, I never saw anyone who looked like you, Jethro. But there was this one time, I saw a young guy, younger than us, who looked really similar to you. He had the hair and the *grrrr*. Doctor Gregory was ushering him into the back offices. When I asked the other patients who he was, one said the kid was Doctor Gregory's son.'

'Oh,' I say. I gaze at the billboard. 'So, you're saying this kid had the…what I've got, the night sickness?'

Paul nods.

'You're not sick, Wolfie,' says Nia.

'Uh, I think I might be a bit sick.' I look at the billboard and Doctor Gregory's oversized head in a new light. 'This guy is trying to do something for his son, and what do I do? I draw a giant body part pointing at his mouth.'

'I should have realised,' says Paul. 'After all those questions about you, I should have put the two things together. But I was dreaming so often, and I only saw the kid once. It makes you think, though, doesn't it?'

'I don't feel sorry for Doctor Gregory,' says Nia. 'I don't care who his son is. I want to do a billboard too. Is there another one that's easier to get to? I could stand on your shoulders, Wolfie.'

I look at Paul. He shrugs. The new colour that was flushing his cheeks has faded a bit.

'There's the one near Dreamer's Row.' I say. I find I don't feel that sorry for Doctor Gregory after all. 'It's not far.'

As we continue along deserted Grey Street I feel unfamiliarly content. What Paul has told us is a weapon I can use should Doctor Gregory hassle me again. But after hearing it I don't feel like fighting him anymore. I don't need revenge on Doctor Gregory. If daylight is really coming to Shyness, his days are already numbered.

'Paul, how much of the dream do you remember? Our dream, that is,' asks Nia.

'A bit. Not all of it,' he says, sounding nervous. 'I remember I would have stayed there trying to talk to Ingrid for the rest of my life. And you saved me again in the river.'

'Does this make any sense to you?' Nia asks me.

'Not really. Sounds interesting, though.' If I had the guts for it I wouldn't mind a peek into Nia's dreams. I'd hate her to see inside my head, though.

'It wasn't interesting, it was pathetic and probably perverted,' Paul says. 'And I feel like there was an important lesson I missed. Something I'm supposed to remember.'

'Don't put girls in lycra,' says Nia. 'That's a lesson for you, right there.'

'Oh god,' says Paul. 'I don't want to know what you mean by that.'

Nia gives him a quick one-armed hug. 'I didn't save you,' she says. 'You saved yourself. You were brave.'

We turn onto a side street, near where I saw the blue people for the first time. The billboard I'm thinking of is right near Ennio's cafe. I don't think Nia will be able to reach it anyway, putting an end to our run of vandalism for the afternoon.

Paul speaks again. 'The strangest thing was seeing Diana's face in the crowd. I haven't see little Di in months,

273

and then she pops up in my subconscious.'

'Jethro's niece?' Nia's interest sparks. 'What does she look like?'

'Tiny, brown hair shaped like a bike helmet. Dresses kooky, little girl kooky. Pink and red and stripes and stuff.'

'Does she have gumboots with rainbows on them?'

'Yeah, they're her favourite.' I answer for Paul. Sometimes Diana won't even take those boots off to go to bed.

'I saw her. She was in the sky as well. I saw her in the sky.' Nia looks up at me, her hair tumbling in unbrushed waves. 'But I don't think that was from Paul's mind, I think it came from mine. I put Diana in the dream.'

'But you've never met her,' I say. 'How could you dream about her?'

'No, but I saw her earlier today in the fake forest, except I didn't know it was her. I just thought she was some cute little kid.'

I halt. 'When?'

'While you were sleeping. I couldn't get back to sleep so I went for a walk in the forest.'

'Are you sure? Maybe it was someone else.'

'No. I saw her this morning, and then again, twice, in the dream. And Paul recognised her.'

Paul chimes in. 'It was Diana, Jethro. I'd recognise her anywhere.'

'See, Wolfie, it makes sense.' Nia hits me lightly in the arm.

I remember trying to call Ortolan and Diana when I woke up. It's possible they were playing in the fake forest, although I've never heard Ortie mention going there. But then there were all those text messages yesterday that Ortie didn't reply to. She's normally pretty good at replying.

'Was she with Ortolan?'

'No, she was with some guy.'

My blood runs ice, even while my voice stays calm. 'Which guy?'

'A man in a suit. I assumed it was her dad.'

Nia's face drops as she realises Diana doesn't have a dad who's alive.

'What did he look like?'

'Just a regular old guy. Kind of graying hair I guess.' Her eyes are already looking scared. She blinks. 'He had this, it was a birthmark, I suppose. A red thing over his eye.'

I'm stuck to the footpath with horror, almost as surely as if my feet had been concreted in. 'Fuck. The darkitect. We have to find her.'

32

Wolfboy punches buttons on his phone, and Paul and I try to cope with the typhoon force of his panic. The effects of Amelia's recovery drink have worn off, and I'm starting to feel flat and queasy. It must be the same for Paul, because he sits at the edge of the road with his head in his hands. Either that or he's sick with worry.

'No answer, no answer, no answer,' repeats Wolfboy, stepping up and down on the gutter. I try to see his face, because I can't talk sense to him if I can't look him in the eye.

'We don't know anything about this guy. Diana didn't seem scared. She was laughing.'

'Shh, I'm trying to think.' Wolfboy clutches at his

hair. 'Doctor Gregory mentioned her. He threatened her. I thought he was bluffing. What if he sent someone for her? We need to start looking.'

'Should we check Birds In Winter first? Or the fake forest? How about we start there?'

'Is there any point? That was almost eight hours ago. If you'd told me at the time maybe we could have done something about it.'

Wolfboy's voice is full of jagged edges. I tell myself it's because he's upset and that I shouldn't take it personally. 'I didn't know at the time who she was. If I did, then of course I would have told you. Let's go to their house then.'

'If anyone was there, they'd pick up the phone.'

I try to keep my voice reasonable. 'Maybe they have loud music on. Or they could be taking a nap.'

Wolfboy finally stops moving. He rests his forehead heavily on my shoulder, which I take as an apology.

'You're right. I don't think I can face going straight to the house. We'll check the forest, then I might be ready to do the shop.'

'I'm coming with you,' says Paul.

We both turn to look at him. My eyebrows raise a notch. The phrase 'death warmed up' doesn't even do justice to Paul's appearance at the moment. I'm feeling crappy, but there's no way I look that bad. His hands are fluttering like butterflies.

'You'll slow us down too much,' Wolfboy snaps.

I make an apologetic face, on Wolfboy's behalf. 'Paul, you don't look so good. Why don't you call Blake, and she can come get you?'

I can tell he doesn't like it, but he nods and gets his phone out.

'Right then,' I grab Wolfboy by the hand and drag him towards the main road. He's gone from paralysis to mania to paralysis in three minutes. 'Let's go.'

Back in the forest again, with Amelia's fur-trimmed hood hugging my face, I feel like I'm in a fairytale, but it's not a good feeling. The wolves are bitey, the witch can't be vanquished and someone might cut off my toes to fit them in a slipper. I can't find the clearing. The torchlight, if anything, makes the flat trees look even weirder and more confusing.

'I'm sure we're close.'

I take us in another circle. Wolfboy's hand burns in mine. You wouldn't think it would be so difficult to find an exercise bike among a bunch of fake trees. I slow down. Deep breaths. Think. I don't want to fail Wolfboy on this. His panic is contagious.

'Sorry for snapping earlier,' he says.

'It's fine.' I'm more worried that I won't be able to find the place where I saw Diana.

I spy a gap in the trees ahead, where they are less dense. There's no such thing as the sound of a footstep in this forest.

The gap becomes the clearing, and there's the white bicycle frame. I speed up to confirm it. The clearing is as empty as the rest of the forest; the bike pedals stationary.

I move closer to inspect a darker speck on the pale wood shavings. It's a stretchy red headband with white polka dots. I pick it up. Wolfboy watches me. Reluctantly I hold up the headband so he can see it.

We run up the middle of the road, my school shoes making slapping sounds on the bitumen. We're in too much of a rush to hold hands, but there's still an invisible thread linking us. The reflective stripes painted down the middle of the road flash by under our feet.

'Little kids lose things all the time,' I say. I'm too busy trying to keep up with Wolfboy to take in the sights, but I'm dimly aware of the darkness to my left, and the lowering daylight to my right.

'You're trying to make me feel better.' Wolfboy's not even out of breath.

'No, I'm not. I'm looking at the facts.'

'I know who Diana was playing with, I told you I've seen that guy before. She doesn't know him. He's probably been stalking the two of them for months.'

Proper dread settles in my stomach. I've been trying to stay positive, but now I'm unsure. I cast my thoughts back to the man in the forest, his strangely stilted, suited manner. He didn't seem like a murderer, but what would I know?

'Are we close?'

Now that we're heading into Panwood it's clear that the day is ending all over the city. The sky is aflame, to match the burning in my legs and lungs. Wolfboy doesn't answer, but we're only halfway along the street when he stops. I see a narrow white shop and a curved porch, heavy with vines. Curling cables spell out *BIRDS IN WINTER* in the window, but the attached fairy lights are dead. The shop looks closed. The blinds on the first floor are drawn.

Now that we're here, Wolfboy doesn't want to go in. He stands, arms by his side. I have to reach up on tiptoes to hook my arms over his shoulders. He crushes me to him and I crush him back.

'I'm glad you're here with me,' he says into my hair.

'Let's check it out.'

I press my lips fleetingly against his, then lead him to the door. Wolfboy rummages in his pockets, before turning to me, hollow-eyed.

'I left my keys at home.'

I bang as loud as I can on the red door with my fist. No answer. Wolfboy puts his ear to it and shakes his head.

He steps into the middle of the road to look up at the first floor. I hit the door again, and try to see through the gauzy material draped in the shop window.

'Nia.'

Wolfboy points to the side of the shop. There's a narrow picket gate to the left, squished in between the shop and the next terrace. The gate is ajar.

'I've never noticed that before, in all the times I've been here,' he says.

The gate grates and complains, but pushes open to reveal a narrow passageway clotted with knee-high weeds. The passage runs the length of the building, which is surprisingly deep. My entire body thumps with adrenaline, and I'm still breathing hard. It seems to me that the weeds have been trampled on recently, but I don't say this to Wolfboy. It's cold in the shadow of the brick wall and the vegetation pulls at my legs. I'm glad when I reach the end.

A large deck extends from the end of the house, over-looking the rambling backyard, and on it stands Diana. Relief floods my system.

'Diana,' I say, before considering whether I'm going to freak her out. She catches sight of me through the deck railing. She doesn't smile, but she doesn't scream either. She's wearing a yellow rain cape that billows.

'Who's there, Diana?'

A man speaks, just as I round the corner and I see that

it's the man from the forest. He walks towards me, with a puzzled expression. I judge the distance between me and Diana, right before I see Ortolan, leaning against the back of the house.

'Nia?' she says, and then she sees Wolfboy behind me. 'Jethro. Why didn't you use your keys?'

'I don't have them on me.' Wolfboy walks up the stairs onto the deck, bristling. 'I've been calling you for hours. Why haven't you answered? I thought something had happened.'

Diana bobs towards him, tucking her hands under her armpits to make chicken wings. Wolfboy gathers her up in his arms and receives lip-smacking kisses all over his face.

'We've had a busy day.' Ortolan is taken aback. Diana squirms and Wolfboy puts her down. 'I'm sorry, I should have checked my phone. It's good you're here, though. You should meet Mr Beechley.'

The man steps forward and I see his face clearly for the first time. He has a kind face close up, weathered, but soft where it counts. His suit is impeccable, his grey hair styled neatly.

'I've met Mr Beechley before, although he didn't tell me his name at the time.' Wolfboy refuses to shake Mr Beechley's outstretched hand.

Ortolan leans around the two men. 'Nia, it's good to see you back in our part of town.'

I creep up the stairs, super-sheepish, and conscious all of a sudden that my tights are speckled with burrs and my hair is tangled beyond hope.

'Hi.' I nod at Mr Beechley. I put my hand in the small of Wolfboy's back, because I can tell he's losing steam fast and probably isn't going to talk again soon. 'Sorry to barge in like this, it's just that we, uh, we thought there was a problem—'

My words dribble away. There's no polite way to say that we thought Mr Beechley kidnapped Diana, and no sane way to say that Diana appeared to me in a dream after I saw her in the forest.

'The forest,' I say to Diana, and to Mr Beechley, glad to have found something concrete to say. 'I saw you there this morning.'

Mr Beechley looks puzzled. Diana has a smirk on her face, though, and I'm willing to bet she did actually spot me after all.

'That's correct,' says Mr Beechley. His voice is radio-presenter pleasant. 'I've been assessing Diana all day.'

'Mr Beechley runs a school.' Ortolan comes forward. 'I'm considering sending Diana there next year. We've been spending some time with him, learning about his teaching methods and seeing if Diana is ready yet.'

'It's a selective school, for exceptional students.' Now that I know who he is, I realise Mr Beechley looks very much like my old school principal. 'I've been doing some tests with Diana to assess her abilities. She's a very special person.'

Diana stands with her stout legs akimbo. 'Basickerly,' she says, 'Mr Beechley wants to see me fly.'

'We did counting and shapes too, as well as drawing and cutting out,' he reminds her.

Diana tugs on Wolfboy's hand. 'I'm not making it up,' she says. 'I can fly.'

'I believe you, Flopsy. No one's saying you can't.'

'Actually, we were about to test this young lady's theory,' says Mr Beechley. 'But I think the deck is too high for our purposes.'

Ortolan rouses herself from smiling at the sight of Diana's hand in Wolfboy's. 'How about the picnic table?'

Mr Beechley walks around the table and chairs nestled in the corner of the deck. He moves two chairs out of the way. Ortolan tests the table with her hands, making sure it doesn't wobble. They're determined to play along.

I turn to Wolfboy. 'Are they for real?'

He shrugs.

'Put me on the table, Jet-ro,' says Diana, so Wolfboy walks her over.

Diana stands on the edge of the slatted table with her arms spread wide and her canary-coloured cape hanging down almost like wings. Behind her is the square shadowy bulk of the house, above that the sky is a mass of streaky tangerine and cherry. The sun is falling fast. Ortolan and Wolfboy stand on either side, ready to catch her. The three of them look like a family. Diana is a miniature version of Ortolan. It's so strange to see them standing side by side. I suddenly miss my mum so much I can't breathe properly. There was never anyone else to help her; it was always and only me and her.

Diana points at me. 'Are you watching me, pretty lady?'

'I'm watching you,' I tell her. I get a Polaroid flash from the dream—Diana bulleting across the sky.

'Pink skies are the best for flying.' Diana bends her knees and the hem of her cape skims her rainbow boots. She jumps, and almost before her feet leave the table Ortolan is there, to sweep her up and whirl her around.

thirty-three

Nia and I sit on the roof of my house, facing each other. The spine is narrow, but it's possible to get almost comfortable by sitting with a leg on either side of the pitched roof.

'When is your mum due back?' I ask.

Nia grips tightly with her knees so she has both hands free to type a message on her phone.

'She missed the train, so late. Later than she expected.'

'We still have time then.'

'A little. I've arranged to meet her in the city when her train arrives at Central.'

'You want me to come with you?'

'To meet my mum?' Nia puts her phone away, and

gives me a goofy look. 'I don't think so. God, no.'

'It'll have to happen eventually.' I wouldn't mind meeting Nia's mum. Well, I would, but if she met me, she might be more relaxed about letting Nia spend time with me. It's a small price to pay.

She smiles. 'Yeah, sure. Maybe in a hundred years or so.'

Now that the panic over Paul and then Diana has subsided, all that's left in my mind is the night we spent together in Amelia's house. I reach out and brush her cheek. 'You're good for me,' I say. 'The light to my shade.'

'Then you're the night to my day. A person needs both, you know.'

She stretches her arms upwards, arches her back, feline. 'It's so beautiful up here. What is it about the stars and the wide open sky that makes everything better?'

I look up as well. 'We don't seem to be able to avoid high places when we're together.'

The moon is still in view but I don't feel as if I'll ever howl again. I'm not sick or angry or sad anymore. I almost lose hold of the roof when my phone rumbles in my pocket. Nia reaches out to steady me.

Private number.

'Hello?'

'Jethro?'

I hesitate, not sure enough to guess. The woman pauses, then realises I'm not going to keep talking.

'Jethro, it's Mum.'

'Oh.' I feel myself tip again and tighten my hold on the tiles. Nia's hand on my leg anchors me. Mum sounds brighter than usual.

'Hi, Mum. Sorry, I didn't—why are you calling?'

It's been a long time since I've had a call from my parents. I can only hear my mum's voice, but my dad's presence hovers just behind her shoulder. He won't talk to me, but he will be listening.

'Can't I call my own son for a chat?'

I don't reply.

'Well, the thing is, we heard what's happening there.'

She could be referring to almost anything. 'What have you heard?'

'Honey, we heard the Darkness is lifting.'

I look at Nia, who stares back curiously, wondering who I'm talking to. Behind her is a backdrop of night, patchwork roofs, stars, dead trees, abandoned towers. The sky might be bleeding purple at the horizon, I don't know.

'You heard wrong,' I say. 'It's still dark.'

288

Acknowledgments

Thank you, always, to my family, for enquiring, listening, supporting and encouraging.

Thanks to my readers-slash-gentle critics Andrew and Nathan, for their enthusiasm and pedantry, and for being willing to travel to the stranger nooks of my imagination.

At the wonderful Text family, special thanks to my editor Alison Arnold, publicist Stephanie Stepan, and rights manager Anne Beilby. Once again, WH Chong has given me a cover more beautiful than I thought was possible.

Thank you to Readings for being thoroughly flexible and understanding employers, who regularly feed my love of books and my bank account.

Thanks to Ange for her creative counselling, writing boot-camp company, illuminating conversation and general all-round care.

I'd like to thank Peter and Juliet for letting us stay twice in their beautiful home in Kennett River during the writing of this book. The words came easier among the koalas and the trees.

Finally, I am very lucky to be part of a like-minded community of friends, writers, readers, bloggers and colleagues who spark my intellect, tickle my fancy, make me laugh and send me off into labyrinthine internet searches. You are all so curious, funny and clever I want to write down everything you say and use it in a book one day.

THIS IS SHYNESS
Leanne Hall

A girl on a mission to forget.
A guy who howls.

In the suburb of Shyness, where the sun doesn't rise
and the border crackles with a strange energy,
Wolfboy meets a stranger at the Diabetic Hotel.

She tells him her name is Wildgirl, and she dares him
to be her guide through the endless night.

But then they are mugged by the sugar-crazed Kidds.
And what plays out is moving, reckless...dangerous.

There are things that can only be said in the dark.
And one long night is time enough to change your life.